Fighting Fantasy: dare you play them all?

1. The Warlock of Firetop Mountain
2. City of Thieves
3. The Citadel of Chaos
4. The Forest of Doom
5. House of Hell
6. The Port of Peril
7. Creature of Havoc
8. Deathtrap Dungeon
9. Appointment with F.E.A.R.
10. Island of the Lizard King
11. Sorcery! 1: The Shamutanti Hills
12. The Gates of Death
13. Caverns of the Snow Witch
14. Sorcery! 2: Kharé: Cityport of Traps
15. Assassins of Allansia

CAVERNS
OF THE
SNOW
WITCH

IAN LIVINGSTONE

SCHOLASTIC

N
ALLANSIA
S
ICEFINGE
CHIANG
MAI
Kaad
PAGA
RED RIVER
Dark Tower
Mirewate
Flax
CATFIS
DOGFISH ISLAND
PORT BLACKSAN
WHI
OYSTER BAY
FIRE ISLAND
SKULL COAST
SOUTHER
BLOOD ISLAND
THE DESERT OF SKULLS

MOUNTAINS
Zengis
Fang
RIVER
KOK
Anvil
PLAINS
Stonebridge
Firetop
Mountain
KAY-PONG
MOONSTONE
HILLS
DARKWOOD
FOREST
Yaztromo's
Tower
RIVER
Largo
Deedle
Water
FOREST OF
SPIDERS
RIVER
SILVER
CHALICE
SILVERTON
Coven
KNOTOAK
WOOD
TROLLTOOTH
PASS
WINDWARD
PLAIN
FOREST
OF YORE
VATER
RIVER
PLAIN
VALE OF
WILLOW
SALAMONIS
TO THE
FLATLANDS
SHAZÂAR
Black
Tower
Vatos
CRAGGEN
HEIGHTS
LEO HARTAS

Scholastic Children's Books
An imprint of Scholastic Ltd
Euston House, 24 Eversholt Street, London, NW1 1DB, UK
Registered office: Westfield Road, Southam, Warwickshire, CV47 0RA
SCHOLASTIC and associated logos are trademarks and/or
registered trademarks of Scholastic Inc.

First published in the UK by Penguin Group, 1984
This edition published in the UK by Scholastic Ltd, 2019

Cover and inside illustrations by Robert Ball, 2019
Map illustration by Leo Hartas, 2017

Fighting Fantasy is a trademark owned by Steve Jackson
and Ian Livingstone, all rights reserved.
Fighting Fantasy Gamebook Concept © Steve Jackson and Ian Livingstone, 1982

ISBN 978 1407 18847 8

Printed by CPI Group (UK) Ltd, Croydon, CR0 4YY
Papers used by Scholastic Children's Books are made
from wood grown in sustainable forests.

1 3 5 7 9 10 8 6 4 2

www.scholastic.co.uk

Official FIGHTING FANTASY website www.fightingfantasy.com

CONTENTS

HOW WILL YOU START YOUR ADVENTURE?
8

BACKGROUND
11

CAVERNS OF THE SNOW WITCH
17

RULES AND EQUIPMENT
201

ADVENTURE SHEET
212

HOW WILL YOU START
YOUR ADVENTURE?

The book you hold in your hands is a gateway to another world – a world of dark magic, terrifying monsters, brooding castles, treacherous dungeons and untold danger, where a noble few defend against the myriad schemes of the forces of evil. Welcome to the world of **FIGHTING FANTASY!**

You are about to embark upon a thrilling fantasy adventure in which **YOU** are the hero! **YOU** decide which route to take, which dangers to risk and which creatures to fight. But be warned – it will also be **YOU** who has to live or die by the consequences of your actions.

Take heed, for success is by no means certain, and you may well fail in your mission on your first attempt. But have no fear, for with experience, skill and luck, each new attempt should bring you a step closer to your ultimate goal.

Prepare yourself, for when you turn the page you will enter an exciting, perilous **FIGHTING FANTASY** adventure where every choice is yours to make, an adventure in which **YOU ARE THE HERO!**

How would you like to begin your adventure?

IF YOU ARE NEW TO FIGHTING FANTASY ...

It's a good idea to read the rules before you start, which appear on pages 201-210.

IF YOU HAVE PLAYED FIGHTING FANTASY BEFORE ...

You'll realize that to have any chance of success, you will need to discover your hero's attributes. You can create your own character by following the instructions on pages 201-202. Don't forget to enter your character's details on the Adventure Sheet which appears on pages 212-213.

ALTERNATIVE DICE

If you do not have a pair of dice handy, dice rolls are printed throughout the book at the bottom of the pages. Flicking rapidly through the book and stopping on a page will give you a random dice roll. If you need to 'roll' only one die, read only the first printed die; if two, total the two dice symbols.

BACKGROUND

Winters in northern Allansia are always cruel and bitter. The snow falls thick and the icy wind blows hard, chilling everybody to the bone. For the past few weeks you have been hired by a merchant called Big Jim Sun to protect his trading caravans as they roll their way slowly north to the frozen outposts. The horse-drawn carts are laden with cloth, utensils, weapons, salted meats, spices and tea, which are traded for furs and ivory carvings made from mammoths' tusks. Big Jim is not usually worried about travelling north, as bandits only attack his caravans on the return journey – he is not alone in recognizing the value of the northern goods.

On this particular trip you are walking ahead of six carts across a frozen lake. In the distance you can see the snow-capped peaks of the Icefinger Mountains jutting out of low cloud. Your destination lies at the base of the mountains where the Northmen meet to trade. Snow is falling, but not too heavily. You stop to prod the ice with your sword to make sure it can bear the weight of carts, when suddenly the shrill call of a hunting horn breaks the silence. You stand up and run back to the carts to talk to Big Jim. He is sitting next to the driver of the second cart, puffing on a long briar pipe. A huge man, with a great bushy beard, Big Jim is obviously a man to be reckoned with. His bright blue eyes scan the horizon, searching for signs of life. In a deep voice he says, 'Sounds like it came from the outpost. Reckon you better go and investigate. Could be trouble. And get back quick.'

You set off straight away towards the outpost at the base of Icefinger Mountains. You arrive two hours later at a scene of ugly carnage. The snow is red with blood and all the wooden huts are smashed and torn down. Six men lie dead, their bodies slashed, their axes at their sides in the snow. Judging by the size of the footprints, the creature that attacked the outpost must have been enormous. There is nothing you can do for the unfortunate Northmen, so you head back towards Big Jim's caravan to report the news. You reach them in an hour, just as the daylight is fading, and relate the terrible events that have befallen the outpost. Big Jim orders the carts to be drawn into a circle to protect his men during the night. A large fire is built into the centre of the circle and you sit down beside it to talk to Big Jim. Everybody is nervous and a guard is posted to watch for signs of movement outside. In a low voice, Big Jim asks you if you will hunt the terrible creature,

for otherwise his business will be ruined forever. You smile and reply that you will track down the beast, but only for a purse of 50 Gold Pieces. Big Jim's jaw drops open, and it takes a great deal of persuasion before he agrees to your demand. The snow finally stops falling as you settle down for the night; sleep is a long time coming, for your mind is active with thoughts of the impending hunt.

When you wake just after dawn, the fire is reduced to dying embers. Wisps of smoke rise gently into the morning mist and not a sound is to be heard. You walk over to where Big Jim is sleeping and tap him on the shoulder. He wakes with a start and you tell him that you are setting off and hope to be back later in the day. You wave to the guard as the snow starts to fall again, and make your way back to the outpost.

YOUR
ADVENTURE
AWAITS!

MAY YOUR STAMINA NEVER FAIL!

NOW TURN OVER...

1

By the time you reach the outpost again, the bodies are blanketed with snow and the beast's footprints are covered over. The visibility is poor as you set off towards the mountains where you hope to find the abominable killer beast. The snow on the mountainside is soft and you sink in up to your knees as you climb slowly up. You soon find yourself at the edge of a crevasse which is spanned by an ice bridge. If you wish to cross the crevasse by the ice bridge, turn to **335**. If you would rather walk around the crevasse, turn to **310**.

2

If you rescued the Genie from the prism, you may call on him now (turn to **14**). If you did not rescue the Genie, you have no defence against the crushing blows of the Crystal Warrior and your quest is over.

3

By some miracle, you are not hit by the heavy chunks of falling ice. When they finally stop crashing around you, you are surprised to see the welcome sight of blue sky above. The three of you waste no time clambering out of the ice cavern, and you find yourselves on the side of the mountain. It is not even snowing and everything looks tranquil. As you climb down the mountain, you tell your friends about Big Jim Sun and the circumstances that led you to enter the caverns of the Snow Witch. You realize that Big Jim would have presumed you were dead; and you decide it is not worth chasing after him to collect your reward for killing the Yeti. Without any further ado you agree to accompany Redswift and Stubb to Stonebridge (turn to **104**).

4

The stake pierces the Snow Witch's heart and her death wail makes you shudder. She starts to decompose, and soon all that is left is a pile of dust on the floor. You see a vague shape in the wall of ice at the end of the chamber, and decide to investigate (turn to **235**).

5

You instinctively clutch the hilt of your sword, as the Healer's words of warning echo through your mind. Roll two dice. If the total is the same or less than your *SKILL* score, turn to **68**. If the total is greater than your *SKILL* score, turn to **185**.

6

Straining with all their might, your friends manage to force your hand against the door. The tip of the dagger sinks into the wood and you are able to release the handle. Feeling quite relieved, you open the door (turn to **285**).

7

Taking the stick from your backpack, you thrust it at the heart of the Snow Witch. If your *SKILL* is higher than 10, turn to **4**. If your *SKILL* is 10 or less, turn to **380**.

8

You quickly gather your thoughts and remember that a Vampire can only be killed by driving a stake through its heart. If you possess a carved rune stick, turn to **7**. If not, turn to **121**.

9

The arrow thuds into the side of the boat. You row as hard as you can towards the far bank, but you are still within the range of the Dark Elf's arrows. You watch him string his bow again and fire. *Test your Luck*. If you are Lucky, turn to **32**. If you are Unlucky, turn to **239**.

10

You panic when you realize that you are not carrying the weapons needed to slay a Vampire. The Snow Witch slowly overcomes her fear of the garlic and gradually gains control of your mind, forcing you to bare your neck in readiness for her to drink your blood. You will be her servant forever in the world of the undead.

11

As soon as you step on to the white footprints, large hailstones the size of walnuts rain down on you. It is impossible to avoid being battered by the heavy ice balls. Lose 2 *STAMINA* points. The shower stops as abruptly as it started when all three of you get past the footprints. Cursing the bewitched caverns you press on down the tunnel (turn to **207**).

12

The iron ball flies through the air and hits the Frost Giant on the temple. His huge frame crumples to the floor like a house of cards. The wooden chest he was lifting breaks open, spilling its contents. You find three ornate rings and a cracked bottle which emits a sweet, scented odour. If you wish to try on any of the rings, turn to **65**. If you would rather walk through to the next tunnel, turn to **338**.

By mid-morning Stubb has become quite excited, knowing that he will soon be home. Seconds later, the thought of his dead friend Morri depresses him and he shakes his fist at the unseen Hill Trolls. An hour later you see distant wisps of smoke rising into the sky. 'Stonebridge!' yells Stubb. He starts to run ahead of you, but suddenly stops when he sees a party of six HILL TROLLS marching towards his village. Screaming a dwarfish battle-cry, he raises his axe and charges at them. You cannot leave your friend to fight them on his own and run forward to fight at his side. Two of the Hill Trolls turn to fight you.

	SKILL	STAMINA
First HILL TROLL	9	10
Second HILL TROLL	9	9

Fight them both at the same time. During each Attack Round, they will both make a separate attack on you, but you must choose which of the two you will fight. Attack your chosen Hill Troll as in a normal battle. Against the other you will throw for your Attack Strength in the normal way, but you will not wound it if your Attack Strength is greater; you must just count this as though you have defended yourself against its blow. Of course, if its Attack Strength is greater, it will wound you. If you defeat them both, turn to **211**.

14

The Genie appears, hovering above the Crystal Warrior. He snaps his fingers and you immediately become invisible. The Crystal Warrior punches the air with his rough quartz fists, but you are able to slip by him unnoticed. By the time the invisibility spell wears off, you are well away from your adversary. Further on, the tunnel ends at a T-junction. If you wish to go left, turn to **150**. If you wish to go right, turn to **368**.

15

The Snow Witch stares at you for a long time before calling out 'Circle.' You smile and unfold your clenched fist, revealing the square metal disc. You have outwitted her and she realizes the consequences. The globe starts to fill with white smoke and suddenly it shatters, the image of the Snow Witch disappears. Her shrill cry fills the cavern, but she is defeated. The three of you slap each other's hands in celebration. However, your joy is short-lived as you hear an ominous rumbling. The ground beneath your feet starts to tremble and huge cracks appear in the ice walls. The roof starts to cave in. Is this the chance to escape that the Snow Witch promised? Test your *LUCK*. If you are Lucky, turn to **3**. If you are Unlucky, turn to **358**.

16

You take careful aim again and throw the dagger at the knob. Test your *LUCK*. If you are Lucky, turn to **120**. If you are Unlucky, turn to **153**.

17

As you draw your sword, the Mountain Elf lets out a shrill battle-cry, pulls back his cloak and grips his sword.

MOUNTAIN ELF   *SKILL 6*   *STAMINA 6*

If the Mountain Elf's *STAMINA* falls to **2**, turn to **305**.

18

The other Bird-men, who were circling above you, fly east after seeing the first Bird-man killed. Frightened that they might return with a huge flock, you decide to run across the plain. The sun is now overhead and you begin to sweat profusely. You become unbearably thirsty and curse the fact that you have not got a water-bottle. You finally reach a water-hole, but you feel like screaming when you see the body of an OGRE lying face down in the water. If you wish to drink the water, turn to **301**. If you would rather resist the temptation to drink, turn to **63**.

19

The Healer is right behind you, urging you to hurry through the cave. You walk on in silence until you see sunlight streaming through a crack at the end of the cave. You see that the crack is just wide enough for you to squeeze through, and you ask the Healer, 'What will happen next?' He calmly replies, 'This is as far as I go. The final part of your ordeal you must face alone. Wearing your mask, you must be at the summit of Firetop Mountain before dawn to watch the sunrise. You must sit cross-legged facing east – you will be totally cured the moment the first rays of sunlight come up over the horizon. If you have something made of silver, we will be able to attract a PEGASUS to fly you there.' If you possess any silver object, turn to **328**. If you do not have any silver, turn to **206**.

20

The tunnel soon ends at a T-junction. Stepping into the cross passage you almost bump into a primitive-looking man wearing furs and carrying a large stone club. He is a CAVE-MAN. You draw your sword and tell Redswift and Stubb to head quickly down the right-hand tunnel while you deal with the Caveman.

CAVE-MAN   *SKILL 8*   *STAMINA 8*

If you win, turn to **141**. You may *Escape* after two Attack Rounds by running along the tunnel to catch up with Redswift and Stubb (turn to **365**).

21

You are now wearing a magic ring which will enable its wearer to resist the effects of freezing cold. Add 1 *LUCK* point. If you have not done so already, you may put on either the silver ring (turn to **159**) or the copper ring (turn to **130**). Alternatively, you may walk through to the next tunnel (turn to **338**).

22

The Mountain Elf shrugs his shoulders and says, 'Well, don't say I didn't warn you – you won't get a chance to change your mind once you are wearing the obedience collar. Follow the tunnel to where it branches and take the right fork. Good luck.' You thank the Elf for his advice and set off again (turn to **136**).

23

The Snow Witch looks surprised and displeased by the defeat of her Zombies. Suddenly she says, 'The game we are going to play is called Discs. You will not win, of course. But in the unlikely event that you do, I will give you the chance to escape. I hope you have remembered to bring along your discs. Without them you lose!' She laughs sadistically at the thought of making up the rules on the spur of the moment. Nevertheless, you must play as directed. If you have any small metal discs, turn to **113**. If you do not possess any discs, turn to **40**.

He puts an arrow in his bow and fires it at you

24

The liquid sends a glow through your body and you feel wonderfully warm. You have swallowed a potion made by the Snow Witch that keeps her followers from feeling the cold. Add 3 *STAMINA* points. The potion also cures frostbite. Any *SKILL* points that you may have lost because of frostbite are now restored. With renewed vigour you walk back out of the cavern (turn to **56**).

25

Now that the snow has stopped falling, the sky is clear and blue. The air is cold and crisp and the snow crunches beneath your feet. Slowly you make your way up the mountainside looking for the cave entrance marker left by the fur trapper. Suddenly you hear a distant rumbling from above – the terrifying sound of an avalanche. *Test your Luck.* If you are Lucky, turn to **163**. If you are Unlucky, turn to **109**.

26

You climb into the boat and push off from the bank. You are about half-way across the river when you hear someone shouting angrily behind you. Looking round you see the irate owner of the boat, a DARK ELF wearing his familiar black hooded cloak. He puts an arrow in his bow and fires it at you. *Test your Luck.* If you are Lucky, turn to **9**. If you are Unlucky, turn to **227**.

27

When you reach the hut, you kick open the door and walk in with your sword drawn. Unfortunately, the hut is empty. The herbalist must have packed hurriedly and fled with your gold. Lose 1 *LUCK* point. You walk back down the path and up the river valley, hoping that you will live long enough to meet the herbalist again (turn to **205**).

28

Time passes slowly but no Goblins appear; the rebel slaves must be winning the battle of the caverns. Eventually you feel fit enough to walk, and, with the help of Stubb, you manage to hobble down the tunnel (turn to **166**).

29

You are soon back at the fork and you turn left into the other branch of the tunnel (turn to **106**).

30

The Death Spell is not working as quickly on you as it is on Redswift. You help him to his feet, apologizing that you made him read the infernal spell. He tells you not to worry about it, he was as good as dead anyway as a slave in the ice caverns. You manage to struggle on for another hour, carrying poor Redswift on your back. Suddenly his fingers dig into your arm and then his whole body relaxes; the Death Spell has won. After burying your elfin friend in a leafy glade, you set off as quickly as you can towards the Moonstone Hills: But you are weak and cannot walk very fast. Lose 1 *SKILL* point and 1 *STAMINA* point The ground becomes steeper as you approach the foothills, and you wonder which way you should go to find the Healer. If you wish to continue east following the river into the hills, turn to **46**. If you would rather cross the river by the rope bridge ahead of you, and walk south along the base of the hills for a while, turn to **385**.

31

Test your *LUCK*. If you are Lucky, turn to **295**. If you are Unlucky, they realize that you are lying and close in on you (turn to **143**).

32

The arrow flies overhead and you reach the far bank before the Dark Elf has time to fire again. You jump out of the boat, gesture at the Dark Elf and set off south across the Pagan Plain towards Stonebridge (turn to **278**).

33

The followers are a group of Goblins, Orcs and Neanderthals. As you make a run for it, the two creatures who are nearest try to stop you. One cracks his whip, trying to wrap it round your legs, while the other aims a dart at you. *Test your Luck*. If you are Lucky, turn to **226**. If you are Unlucky, turn to **340**.

34

Taking the stick from your backpack, you thrust it at the heart of the Snow Witch. If your *SKILL* is higher than 10, turn to **4**. If your *SKILL* is 10 or less, turn to **123**.

35

Once again your friends fail to overcome the power of the dagger. You watch with horror as your arm rises and plunges the dagger into your own chest. Your adventure ends here.

36

The front door of the hut is frozen shut and you have to batter it with your shoulder to open it. There is only one room inside the hut containing the belongings of a fur trapper. Traps, furs and sacks are stacked in a corner of the room. A wooden bed, a table and chair and some cooking utensils show sign of recent use, and the ashes in the fire are still warm. If you wish to put some logs on the fire and warm up the cold stew in one of the pans, turn to **118**. If you would rather leave the hut and continue your quest, turn to **192**.

Its face is ashen and its eyes are just two grey folds of skin

The figure in front of you steps forward again; it is holding a lantern and when it gets closer you see its horrific features. Its face is ashen and its eyes are just two grey folds of skin sunken in their sockets. You have entered the dark domain of a NIGHT STALKER and you must fight it.

NIGHT STALKER   SKILL 11   STAMINA 8

During each round of combat, you must reduce your Attack Strength by 2 because you are not used to fighting in the dark. If you win, turn to **306**.

38

Even though it is quite cool walking along the bank of the Red River, you start to sweat and feel dizzy. You look at Redswift and he, too, looks far from well. His face is white and his eyes look dark and sunken. 'Sit down,' says Redswift in a laboured voice. You gratefully stop and collapse on to the grass, quite worried now as your heart is beating very fast. 'Do you remember walking through the caverns of the Snow Witch and arriving at a door with a piece of parchment nailed to it? You could not understand what was written on it and asked me to read it. It was a Death Spell and we are now both doomed. It is starting to work on us sooner than I expected. We have to find the old man of the hills that they call the Healer. Only he can save us now. But I fear it may be too late already. My legs are so weak, I don't know if I'll be able to stand again.' If you drank the Potion of Health that belonged to the Dark Elf, turn to **30**. If you did not drink this Potion, turn to **367**.

39

Thrusting your leg out to the side, you kick the nearest Goblin in the stomach. He doubles up, and an upper-cut to the jaw sends him crashing to the floor. The other Goblin lunges forward and tries to stab you with his dagger. *Test your Luck*. If you are Lucky, turn to **240**. If you are Unlucky, turn to **386**.

40

Feeling cheated because you have lost the game before it even started, you draw your sword, intent on smashing the Snow Witch's globe (turn to **244**).

41

You tread carefully over the bridge. Safely across the crevasse, you continue your slow trek through the snow (turn to **212**).

42

You pull the straps off your shoulders and watch your backpack disappear under the water. You have lost all your gold, your possessions and any remaining Provisions. Lose 2 *LUCK* points. The strong current drags you down river, and all you can do is try to save yourself from drowning. *Test your Luck.* If you are Lucky, turn to **201**. If you are Unlucky, turn to **280**.

43

You pick up your sword from the floor and search through the clothing of the Goblins. You find and take their two daggers, some salted fish, a candle and 2 Gold Pieces. The metal collars round their necks have stopped glowing, but you cannot remove them. Wondering if any more traps lie beyond the ice pit, you try to decide which way to head. If you wish to continue down the tunnel, turn to **88**. If you would rather walk back to where the tunnel forked and turn left along the other branch, turn to **29**.

44

The energy bolt which hits you is too much of a shock for your body to bear. You are knocked to the ground and black out. You do not wake up again and your adventure ends here.

45

You examine the wooden chest lying on the floor and decide to prise it open with your sword. Inside you find three ornate rings and a cracked bottle which emits a sweet odour. If you wish to try on any of the rings, turn to **65**. If you would rather walk through to the next tunnel, turn to **338**.

46

The river narrows and the ground becomes steeper. As you climb, you feel yourself becoming weaker by the minute. Lose 1 *STAMINA* point. You walk past a large hollow tree stump, paying it no attention, until you notice a thick vine, which is tied to its roots and runs up over the edge of the stump. You look inside the hollow stump and see the vine disappearing into its black depths. Will you:

Pull the vine?	Turn to **312**
Climb down the vine?	Turn to **394**
Keep on walking up the river valley?	Turn to **119**

47

It takes half an hour of hard walking to reach the end of the crevasse. You are now able to climb further up the mountain. The steep climb and the swirling snow combine to make the going slow (turn to **337**).

48

When you pick it up, the orb starts to get warmer and its colours change rapidly and swirl around; Redswift and Stubb back away, telling you to put it down. Will you:

Keep hold of the orb?	Turn to **275**
Place it gently on the floor?	Turn to **117**
Throw it down the tunnel?	Turn to **318**

49

As soon as you step into the tunnel, an iron grille drops down behind you, barring your retreat. It is impossible to lift and there is nothing you can do but find out what lies at the end of the tunnel. You soon arrive at another iron grille which blocks your way forward. Beyond the grille the tunnels turn left. On the wall opposite, you see a knob which you realize must be pressed to lift the iron grille. Unfortunately it is beyond your reach, even if you stretch out with your sword. If you have one or more daggers, turn to **234**. If you have no daggers, turn to **393**.

50

As you approach the fire, you smell the delicious aroma of a duck being roasted. You draw your sword and walk warily forward. Suddenly a sinewy man with long hair and a beard jumps out from behind a rock, screaming at the top of his voice. He is wearing animal furs and carrying a stone club which he raises to attack you. You must fight the WILD HILL MAN.

WILD HILL MAN   *SKILL 6*   *STAMINA 5*

If you win, turn to **320**. You may Escape after two Attack Rounds by running back across the rocks to the north bank of the river (turn to **364**).

51

The energy bolt gives your system a terrible shock. You are knocked to the ground by its force. Lose 1 *SKILL* point and 4 *STAMINA* points. If you are still alive, turn to **336**.

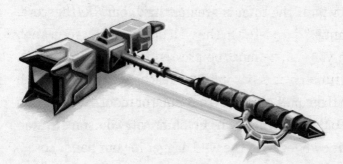

52

You remember an old legend that ground minotaur horn is the only substance that can stop a metamorphosis spell from working. You quickly sprinkle some on the growing creature, and relax a little as it shrinks back to a white rat again. The legend was true! Intrigued by the open sarcophagus, you decide to walk over and examine it (turn to **297**).

53

Nobody replies to your call. If you wish to enter the cave, turn to **246**. If you would rather go back down into the gorge, turn to **355**.

54

You light the candle and look across the pit. It is about 15 metres wide and the log is quite narrow. The Healer tells you to walk across it as soon as you are ready. Roll two dice. If the total is the same or less than your *SKILL* score, turn to **91**. If the total is greater than your *SKILL* score, turn to **78**.

55

When you pull the dagger from the door, it suddenly takes on a will of its own. Involuntarily you start to stab at your own leg with the wild dagger in your hand. Lose 2 *STAMINA* points. Redswift and Stubb run to your aid and try to force your hand to stab the door in order to trap the dagger. *Test your Luck*. If you are Lucky, turn to **6**. If you are Unlucky, turn to **236**.

56

You walk past the entrance tunnel on your left and continue on down the main tunnel (turn to **395**).

57

As you walk away the Dwarf calls out to his god to curse you. Lose 2 *LUCK* points. You walk past the junction and along the other branch of the tunnel, the cries of the Dwarf ringing in your ears (turn to **125**).

58

Lying between the stunted bushes, you listen to the noise of the thundering hooves growing louder. Bending back a branch, you see four CENTAURS gallop by, each armed with a bow and a quiver of arrows. You lie quite still until the sound of their hooves fades. When you are certain that they are out of sight, you stand up and continue your journey south (turn to **278**).

*He is made of quartz which has been animated
by the Snow Witch's sorcery.*

59

Before you stands a CRYSTAL WARRIOR, one of the Snow Witch's personal guardians who has been sent to deal with you. He is made of quartz which has been animated by the Snow Witch's sorcery. Edged weapons will not harm the Crystal Warrior – your sword is useless! If you possess a war-hammer you may succeed in smashing the Crystal Warrior to pieces.

CRYSTAL WARRIOR   *SKILL* 11   *STAMINA* 13

If you do not possess a war-hammer, turn to **2**. If you win, turn to **148**.

60

The Snow Witch climbs out of the sarcophagus and walks towards you with her mouth wide open. Her gaze is powerful and you hear a voice in your mind telling you to drop your sword and loosen your collar. Roll two dice. If the total is the same or less than your *SKILL* score, turn to **8**. If the total is higher than your *SKILL*, turn to **116**.

61

As you walk along, the Elf introduces himself. 'My name is Redswift, and he is known as Stubb,' he says, pointing to the smiling Dwarf. 'We met here as slaves in the service of the vile Snow Witch. We both now hope to return to our villages. I live in the Moonstone Hills and Stubb comes from Stonebridge. If we manage to escape from these infernal caverns, you are more than welcome to come and stay with us. Stonebridge is on the way to my village in the hills. It's also a long way off.' Before Redswift can continue, Stubb shouts, and points to an orb lying on the floor. It is made of glass and in the torchlight it seems to glow with swirling colours. 'Leave it,' commands Redswift, 'we do not need it and it could be a trap.' If you wish to ignore Redswift's advice and pick up the orb, turn to **48**. If you would rather keep on walking, turn to **166**.

62

The Zombie picks up a club from behind the door and shuffles forward to fight you.

ZOMBIE   *SKILL* 6   *STAMINA* 6

If you win, turn to **200**. You may *Escape* after two Attack Rounds by running back to the junction and going straight on down the tunnel (turn to **150**).

63

Your thirst makes you weary. Lose 1 STAMINA point. However, you do not wish to risk drinking the water (turn to **96**).

64

The great wall of snow sweeps you down the mountain. Your head smashes against a rock, knocking you unconscious. By the time the avalanche comes to a halt in a gully, you are buried deep under the snow. Icefinger Mountains have claimed another victim.

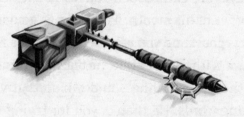

65

Having rubbed the bottle and sniffed your fingers, you decide that it is only perfume inside. You examine the three rings and decide which one to put on your finger. Will you:

Put on the gold ring?	Turn to **21**
Put on the silver ring?	Turn to **159**
Put on the copper ring?	Turn to **130**

66

Taking the shield has unleashed the fury of an AIR ELEMENTAL. An expanding whirlwind thunders down the tunnel. You try to stand your ground, awaiting its terrible impact. Seconds later its ferocious power hits you, and debris caught up in it hurtles towards you. *Test your Luck.* If you are Lucky, turn to **294**. If you are Unlucky, turn to **160**.

67

You kneel down beside the fur trapper and turn him over slowly. His eyes are barely open and blood trickles down from the corner of his mouth. The Yeti has gouged deep wounds in his chest and you realize that there is no hope of saving him. With a great effort he reaches up and grabs you round the neck, pulling you down so that you can hear his dying words. He thanks you for trying to save him, and insists on telling you his secret. In terrible pain he struggles to whisper his story. He tells you that he has lived in the mountains for most of his life, hunting animals and trading their furs, but for the last five years he has been searching for the legendary Crystal Caves. These caves have been cut out of a glacier by the followers of the Snow Witch, a beautiful yet evil sorceress, who is trying to use her dark powers to bring on an ice age so that she can rule supreme over the whole world. The entrance to the Crystal Caves is high up on this very mountain. It is open, but hidden by an illusion. The unfortunate fur trapper found it by accident only yesterday, when he saw one of the Snow Witch's warriors seemingly walk straight through an ice wall and disappear. The trapper left a piece of fur hanging over the entrance so that he could find it again the next day. Sadly, the Yeti has put an end to his hopes. He asks you to enter the caves to slay the vile Snow Witch and leave her followers without their leader. There are legends about great treasures being frozen into the wall of the Snow Witch's lair which would provide ample reward. The fur trapper suddenly grips you hard and then falls back silently into the snow – he's dead. You cover him with snow, before deciding what to do. 50 Gold Pieces await you if you return with evidence of the Yen's death to Big Jim Sun; but the thought of a quest through the Crystal Caves beneath Icefinger Mountains excites you, and you decide to set off to find them (turn to **25**).

68

Between her screams the Banshee tells you that you are going to die. However, the Healer's concoction enables you to resist the temptation to draw your sword to silence her, and you manage to pass by her unharmed (turn to **19**).

69

After putting the coins carefully into a hidden pocket, the old man tells you to be careful of two things if you are travelling south to Stonebridge. Firstly, the nearest water-hole has been poisoned; and secondly, there are lots of Hill Trolls gathering to the north of Stonebridge. He bids you good luck and farewell and walks off. Stubb urges you to set off as quickly as possible, worried about the possible attack on Stonebridge by the Hill Trolls (turn to **348**).

70

The Mountain Elf laughs and says he never puts on any weight, but if he was fortunate enough to be able to take off his collar he might try to run away. He has hardly finished the sentence when he screams in pain. He tries in vain to pull the obedience collar from his neck, begging forgiveness at the top of his voice from an unseen master. He finally stops screaming and slumps to the floor, his face dripping with sweat. You ask him if he is all right, but he does not respond. Lose 1 *LUCK* point. You decide to leave him and press on down the tunnel (turn to **241**).

71

The man springs out of his chair and says, 'Indeed I am. What ails you, stranger?' You tell the old man about your adventures in the ice caverns and the spell that is slowly destroying you. The old man smiles and says, 'Death Spells? They are easy to counteract. You just need a jar of my special mixed herbs, a bargain at only 50 Gold Pieces.' You are surprised that the man wants to charge you money to save your life, but he seems quite adamant. If you wish to pay the man for the herbs, turn to **149**. If you would rather threaten him, turn to **390**.

72

You pretend to give up the fight and then suddenly leap at the Illusionist. Catching him momentarily off guard, you manage to snatch the prism out of his hands and throw it on to the floor. It shatters into tiny pieces and the Illusionist turns and flees into the skull mouth, screaming at the top of his voice. Smoke rises from the shattered fragments of the prism, and forms itself into the shape of a bald fat man – a Genie! Hovering in mid-air, he bows and thanks you for releasing him. He tells you that if you call on him, he will make you invisible, just once, as a token of his gratitude. Without saying another word, the image shimmers and disappears. You now have to decide which way to head. Will you:

Enter the tunnel to your left?	Turn to **266**
Enter the tunnel with the skull mouth?	Turn to **288**
Enter the tunnel to your right?	Turn to **49**

73

Unfortunately you draw the short straw. Lose 1 *LUCK* point. As soon as you touch the casket's handle, it comes to life. An ASP wraps itself around your hand and, before you can shake it off, it sinks its poisonous fangs into your wrist. Lose 4 *STAMINA* points and 1 *SKILL* point. If you are still alive, you manage to stagger down the tunnel (turn to **20**).

74

You blow into the flute and a jolly tune comes from it without your having to play a note. You decide to put the magic flute in your backpack. If you have not done so already you may:

Read the runes on the stick	Turn to **345**
Smell the rose	Turn to **317**
Read the book	Turn to **356**

If you do not wish to do any of the above, you may leave the cave and turn left into the tunnel (turn to **198**).

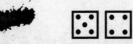

Peering into the cave, you see that it runs deep into the side of the hill. Torches cast an eerie light inside the cave, illuminating wooden carvings and masks that are hanging on the walls. You step inside and see a robed figure sitting on the floor with its back to you. Without turning round, the mysterious person says, 'I am the Healer. If you have come to be healed, stand before me now.' Your heart beats, faster as you walk over to stand in front of him. Before you is a man who is horribly disfigured; his body is terribly twisted, but he sits there proudly, although pain registers on his face. You tell him that you have been cursed with a Death Spell and have come to be cured. The Healer nods his head and says, 'The power of a Death Spell is difficult to destroy. I have only managed to break it once, and it wasn't easy. A ritual has to be performed which you might not survive. Still, you must try. I will help you as much as I can. First, you must place a Mask of Life over your face to halt the spread of the Death Spell. If you survive the initial battle between life and death, you will be able to face the second stage of the reversal process.' The Healer then takes a strange mask off the wall, carved to symbolize the sun. As you place it over your face, you feel as though your body is being torn apart. Roll 1 die and subtract that number from your *STAMINA* score. If you are still alive, turn to **258**.

76

As soon as they see that their leader has been killed, the other Centaurs retreat. You stop Redswift and Stubb from chasing after them. If you do not already possess a shield, you may take the one lying on the ground next to the Centaur leader. Add 1 *SKILL* point. If you wish to try on the Centaur's helmet, turn to **362**. If you would rather leave it and set off immediately for Stonebridge, turn to **278**.

77

Are you carrying a spear? If you are, turn to **391**. If you do not have a spear, turn to **378**.

78

You are half-way across the log when suddenly you panic and start to wobble from side to side. Losing your footing, you fall off the log and plunge headlong down into the deep pit. You hit the stone floor at considerable speed and are killed instantly.

79

The water looks harmless enough, but you do not relish the thought of being wet as well as cold. But you have no choice, you must walk under the gentle waterfall. As you do so, you suddenly notice your clothes are beginning to smoulder. You start to run as you realize that it is not water dripping down, but deadly acid; a trap no doubt devised by the evil Snow Witch to deter runaway servants or slaves. You cry out in pain as the acid burns into your skin. Lose 4 *STAMINA* points. If you are still alive, turn to **383**.

80

The Minstrel looks amazed that you are interested in his music. He stops playing and says, 'You must be new here, as the ignorant scum who live round here – apart from our beloved Snow Queen of course – will not listen to my music. The fools, if only they knew what fortune I could bring them with my songs. Stranger, I can play a song for you that will heal your wounds. Listen carefully and watch. Later tell that rabble about it and perhaps they will come to respect me and my music.' The Minstrel then starts to play a soothing tune and you watch amazed as one of your wounds heals. Add 4 *STAMINA* points. 'Come back again for more treatment some time,' he says, looking pleased with himself. You thank him and leave his cave to continue along the tunnel (turn to **111**).

81

You dive under the outcrop as the snow crashes down all around. Pressing yourself as close as you can against the ice-covered wall of your shelter, you wait until the avalanche has passed by. With a sigh of relief you set off again in search of the Crystal Caves (turn to **363**).

His skin is a sickly grey-white colour

82

You just manage to keep your head above the surface of the water, but you are unable to swim to the bank. *Test your Luck*. If you are Lucky, turn to **201**. If you are Unlucky, turn to **280**.

83

A man comes to the door. His skin is a sickly grey-white colour. His vacant eyes and slow movements are definitely those of a mindless ZOMBIE. If you wish to attack him, turn to **62**. If you wish to run back to the junction and head straight on, turn to **150**.

84

The energy bolt slams into your chest. If your *STAMINA* total is 10 or less, turn to **44**. If it exceeds 10 in total, turn to **51**.

85

By the time you reach the top of the hill, you are panting very heavily. Lose 1 *STAMINA* point. You are so exhausted, that you do not look about you, and only hear Ash's warning cry as a DEATH HAWK dives down to attack you. Ash fires an arrow at the bird of prey. Ash's *SKILL* is 9. Roll two dice. If the total is the same or less than Ash's *SKILL*, turn to **175**. If the total is greater than Ash's *SKILL*, turn to **238**.

86

The Goblins release the rope and stand at the top of the pit, laughing at your useless attempt to trick them. Your predicament is now worse than ever; trapped at the bottom of an ice pit without even your sword. Lose 2 *LUCK* points. You sigh and call to the Goblins, asking them to catch the rope as you throw it up to them again. They take hold of it and you climb up out of the pit. The Goblins are dressed in furs and are also wearing glowing metal collars round their necks. They motion you to walk back down the tunnel, urging you on with the points of their daggers. You realize that you are doomed unless you try to escape. If you wish to fight them with your bare hands, turn to **39**. If you would rather try to run away, turn to **102**.

87

As soon as you step on to the black footprints you feel a strange sensation. Your whole body starts to vibrate and your legs feel so weak that you think you are about to collapse. You press on resolutely, but when you step past the final footprint you still feel as though your body has been drained of some of its strength. Lose 1 *SKILL* point and 3 *STAMINA* points. Cursing the bewitched caverns you press on down the tunnel (turn to **207**).

88

The tunnel continues for some distance before opening out into a circular cave. Another tunnel leads out of the cave directly opposite. You are suddenly met by a strange sight – there are two small pools in the floor with steam gently rising from them; protruding from one pool is the hilt of a sword and, from the other, the shaft of a spear. The frozen body of an Orc lies against the wall, its arm rigid and pointing towards the sword. As you approach the pools you see a rhyme carved in the ice floor which reads:

> Sword or spear
> Strength or fear
> How to choose
> Win or lose.

You stand and ponder the rhyme, trying to decide what to do. Will you:

Draw out the sword from its pool?	Turn to **237**
Pull out the spear from its pool?	Turn to **250**
Walk directly through the cave into the tunnel opposite?	Turn to **221**

89

Test your Luck. If you are Lucky, turn to **331**. If you are Unlucky, turn to **103**.

90

Redswift and Stubb are not injured by the falling ice and they help you to your feet. Above, you are surprised to see the welcome sight of blue sky. The three of you waste no time clambering out of the ice cavern, and you find yourselves on the side of the mountain. It is not even snowing and everything looks tranquil. As you climb down the mountain, you tell your friends about Big Jim Sun and the circumstances that led you to the caverns of the Snow Witch. You realize that Big Jim would have presumed you were dead; and you decide it is not worth chasing after him to collect your reward for killing the Yeti. Without any further ado you agree to accompany Redswift and Stubb to Stonebridge (turn to **104**).

91

Walking slowly and carefully, you reach the other side of the pit, much to your relief. The Healer walks casually across the log as though the pit was not there. 'Good,' he says, 'now you must prepare yourself for the next stage. In order to survive, you must be totally calm. If you have a dragon's egg, I can make you a relaxing concoction.' If you possess a dragon's egg, turn to **359**. If you are not carrying a dragon's egg, turn to **271**.

92

You walk round a large boulder and see a huge man sleeping in the shade. He is lying on top of some animal skins, snoring loudly. His two-handed battleaxe lies propped up against the boulder. He is a BARBARIAN and it would be foolish to wake him up, so you decide to tiptoe past him. If you are wearing elfin boots, turn to **128**. If you are wearing ordinary boots, turn to **374**.

93

You manage to step out of the way of the chest which comes flying towards you. It smashes against the wall and breaks open, spilling its contents on the floor. The Frost Giant lumbers towards you, intent on killing you, but you are ready with your sword.

FROST GIANT   SKILL 10   STAMINA 10

You may *Escape* after two Attack Rounds by running out of his lair into the next tunnel (turn to **338**). If you win, turn to **182**.

94

You stumble to the left and inadvertently step on one of the white footprints (turn to **11**).

The bloodied body of a Dwarf lies propped up against it

95

The Gnome runs up to you and shouts, 'Get out, dinner will not be ready for another two hours. You'll hear the bell. Mind you, you look a little worse for wear, so you can have this stale cake if you wish.' The Gnome points at a piece of cake lying on the table. If you wish to take the cake and leave, turn to **290**. If you would rather attack the Snow Witch's servants, turn to **187**.

96

The three of you set off to the south, worried about the shortage of water. Stubb tries to offer some comfort by saying that you should reach Stonebridge in less than a day. He says that he is surprised that he hasn't seen any of his fellow Dwarfs by now. 'Oh yes we have,' says Redswift solemnly, 'but you won't want to see them like that.' He points to a boulder about 50 metres west. The bloodied body of a Dwarf lies propped up against it, his head has slumped forward, and he is motionless. His axe is still in his hand, and whoever or whatever attacked him cannot be far away. Stubb runs up to the Dwarf wailing in grief. 'It's Morri the Ironsmith,' he says. 'This looks like the work of Hill Trolls. Let's bury Morri and get to Stonebridge as quickly as possible to tell them this terrible news.' Here, take Morri's water-bottle. He won't need it now.' You gulp down the water and are at last refreshed. Add 1 *STAMINA* point. After marking

Morri's grave with his axe and helmet, you set off again for Stonebridge (turn to **110**).

97

There is no writing in the book, just a recess cut in the pages which holds a talisman on a golden chain. The talisman is a jade frog. If you wish to put the chain around your neck, turn to **327**. If you would prefer to leave it in the book, you may, if you have not done so already, do one of the following:

Blow the flute	Turn to **74**
Read the runes on the stick	Turn to **345**
Smell the rose	Turn to **317**

If you do not wish to do any of the above, you may leave the cave and turn left into the tunnel (turn to **198**).

98

Still suffering from the effects of the energy bolt, you have to decide quickly what to do next. If you wish to stand up and run on, turn to **262**. If you would rather try to smash the globe with your sword, turn to **244**.

99

The Illusionist laughs out loud as your sword merely cuts through one of his images and his dagger plunges into your shoulder. Lose 2 *STAMINA* points. Turn to **279**.

100

The Elf asks you why you are looking for the Healer. You tell him about your battles in the ice caverns, the Death Spell and how poor Redswift met his end. 'Redswift!' cries the Elf. 'He's my brother!' He explains that his name is Ash and he never knew that his brother had been enslaved by the Snow Witch. Suddenly, saddened by the news of Redswift's death, he walks away and stands silently in the sunlight. After a few minutes, he says, "I will help you to find the Healer but you will have to face him alone, because he will only make contact with the sick. He was disfigured and cursed with disease and pain by The Dark Ones, the evil spirits of the night, for ridding a wizard named Nicodemus of a Death Spell they had cast on him. Now he practises his work in the solitude of the hills. Follow me, it looks as if we have no time to lose.' Ash walks ahead of you, constantly alert for danger. You climb up the valley for an hour before reaching a rope bridge which spans the river. Ash says that you will have to cross the bridge. You tell him that you will have to rest first as the Death Spell continues to drain your life force. Lose 1 *STAMINA* point. Later you tell Ash that you are ready to continue and step on to the bridge. You are about half-way across when you suddenly hear voices shouting. You look around and see two HILL TROLLS cutting the ropes which secure the bridge to its supports. You hurry as fast as you can towards the far bank. *Test your Luck.* If you are Lucky, turn to **273**. If you are Unlucky, turn to **181**.

101

Lying at the bottom of the red pot is a square metal disc which you decide to put in your backpack. If you now wish to look inside the grey pot, turn to **344**. If not, you may leave the cavern by the opposite door (turn to **176**).

102

The Goblins call 'Halt!' But you keep on running. They both take aim and throw their daggers at you. Roll one die. If you roll a 1 or 2, turn to **140**. If you roll a 3 or 4, turn to **330**. If you roll a 5 or 6, turn to **245**.

103

The Mountain Elf looks surprised, and asks why you are not wearing your obedience collar. You see that he is wearing a metal collar round his neck which glows in the semi-darkness, and realize that it must be the collar he is talking about. If you wish to reply that you have put on weight recently and are having your collar widened, turn to **70**. If you would rather attack the Elf before he raises the alarm, turn to **382**.

104

Your journey south is long and arduous, but your determination to leave Icefinger Mountains behind you spurs you on. Two days after leaving the ice caverns, you reach the River Kok. Fifty miles up-river lies Fang, the town where Baron Sukumvit's notorious Deathtrap Dungeon awaits its challengers each year for the Trial of Champions. However, at this time of year Fang is unlikely to be more interesting than any other river town. You decide against going there and walk down-river to find a bridge or a boatman. After walking for half an hour along the bank of the wide, dirty-brown river, you see a man asleep aboard a raft moored to the bank. You shout to him and ask him to ferry you across. He tells you to go away as he is too tired to work today. If you wish to offer him 10 Gold Pieces to make him change his mind, turn to **315**. If you would rather walk on, turn to **131**.

A neanderthal is stripping the skin off a moose

105

Ash waits for an opportunity to shoot and fires another arrow at close range. This time he does not miss, and the Death Hawk plunges to the ground with an arrow protruding from its breast. The other side of the hill slopes down into a gorge and Ash tells you that you must now journey alone to meet the Healer. He tells you to walk east up the gorge until you see the head of a Phoenix carved in the rock. The Healer lives in a cave in the side of the hill above the carved rock. You thank Ash for his help and walk slowly down the hill into the gorge. At the bottom you follow Ash's instructions and turn left up the gorge (turn to **252**).

106

Further ahead, in the left-hand wall of the tunnel, you see a gap. You walk up to it and peer round to see a cave in which a NEANDERTHAL is stripping the skin off a moose making it ready for the large simmering stew-pot behind him. He is working very slowly and is being yelled at by the GNOME cook who is wearing a white apron and waving a wooden spoon in the air. If you wish to enter the crude kitchen, turn to **95**. If you would rather creep past the entrance, turn to **267**.

107

You stumble, but manage to avoid treading on either the white or the black footprints. Regaining your balance, you walk on between the footprints (turn to **207**).

108

The followers pick you up and carry you over to a circle of ice, dyed blue, in which the effigy stands. Amid wails and wild shouting, they throw you into the blue circle. The effigy immediately jerks its frozen limbs into motion – you have unleashed the power of an ICE DEMON.

ICE DEMON   *SKILL 9*   *STAMINA 11*

In addition to its normal attack, throw one die every Attack Round for the jet of freezing gas that shoots out from its nostrils. On a roll of 1, 2 or 3, the gas will hit you and reduce your *STAMINA* by 1 point, but on a roll of 4, 5 or 6, the gas will miss you. If you win, turn to **184**.

109

You look up and see great cascades of snow tumbling down the mountainside. With horror you realize that you are standing in the path of the avalanche. You look around and see an outcrop under which you could shelter. The approaching mass of snow is no more than a hundred metres away and you struggle to run for cover. Roll two dice. If the total is the same or less than your *SKILL* score, turn to **81**. If the total is greater than your *SKILL* score, turn to **371**.

110

Night is approaching and you decide to camp in the shelter of some rocks and bushes, despite Stubb's plea to carry on. You build a fire and settle down to sleep. Redswift takes the first watch, *Test your Luck*. If you are Lucky, turn to **399**. If you are Unlucky, turn to **251**.

111

In the distance you can hear chanting voices; soon the tunnel ends at the entrance to a large cavern. Kneeling down before an ice effigy in the shape of a demon, with their hooded faces pressed to the ice floor in worship, are ten of the Snow Witch's followers. There are two exits from the cave, one straight ahead and one to your right. If you wish to pretend to be one of the worshippers and walk boldly into the cavern, turn to **300**. If you would rather creep cautiously into the cavern, turn to **283**.

112

If you have a sling and wish to use it against the Frost Giant, turn to **373**. If you would rather fight him with your sword, turn to **292**.

113

The Snow Witch quickly explains the rules of her game; she tells you to choose a disc and conceal it in your clenched fist. She will call out a shape. A square beats a circle. A circle beats a star. And a star beats a square. If you win, you will be given a chance to escape. If you lose, you will die. If you both choose the same shape, you will play again. Your life depends on your next decision. Now you must make your choice. Of course, if you do not possess all three discs, your choice will be limited. Will you:

Conceal the square disc?   Turn to **15**
Conceal the circular disc?   Turn to **152**
Conceal the star disc?   Turn to **392**

114

You manage to keep control of your mind and pick up the stick again. This time you thrust it at the Snow Witch's heart with even more determination (turn to **4**).

115

Through the trees to your left, you see a tall man with pointed ears and fair hair. He is wearing a green cloak and he is busy carving arrow shafts with his knife. He is an ELF, similar in appearance to Redswift. If you wish to ask him if he knows where the Healer lives, turn to **100**. If you would rather attack him with your sword, turn to **397**.

116

You find yourself obeying her command. You loosen your collar and bare your neck in readiness for her to drink your blood. You will be her servant forever in the world of the undead.

117

Expecting something disastrous to happen, Redswift and Stubb shrink back when you place the orb on the ground. But nothing happens except that the orb starts to glow again. You shrug your shoulders and soon catch up with your two companions (turn to **166**).

118

The fire is soon roaring and crackling in the hearth. The heat of the flames radiates through your body and you revel in the warmth. The stew is delicious and you feel your strength returning. Add 3 *STAMINA* points. With renewed energy, you decide to leave the hut to continue your quest (turn to **192**).

119

To your left, you see a narrow footpath leading from the bank of the river into the trees. If you wish to walk up the footpath, turn to **168**. If you would rather go on up the valley, turn to **205**.

120

The dagger hits the knob and the iron grille slowly starts to rise. Add 1 *LUCK* point. You waste no time – you run under the grille, turn left and keep going until you arrive at a crossroads. There are no signs of life either from straight ahead or from the branch to 1| your left, but advancing towards you along the right-hand runnel is a strange humanoid (turn to **59**).

121

You panic as you realize that you are not carrying the weapons needed to slay a Vampire. The Snow Witch gradually gains control of your mind and forces you to bare your neck in readiness for her to drink your blood. You will be her servant forever in the world of the undead.

122

The energy bolt which hits you, gives your system a terrible shock. You are knocked to the ground by its force. Lose 1 *SKILL* point and 4 *STAMINA* points. If you are still alive, turn to **322**.

He commands you to turn back

123

The Snow Witch manages to overcome her fear of garlic and knocks the stick out of your hand. Her gaze is powerful and you hear a voice in your mind telling you to drop the garlic and loosen your collar. Roll two dice. If the total is the same or less than your *SKILL* score, turn to **114**. If the total is higher than your *SKILL*, turn to **134**.

124

When you land on the third rock, your foot slips and you fall into the river. You are swept downstream and you are too weak to swim against the fast-flowing current. If you are carrying 400 or more Gold Pieces, turn to **381**. If you are carrying less than 400 Gold Pieces, turn to **82**.

125

The tunnel through the glacier soon leads into the mountainside itself and the walls change from ice to bare rock. You enter a large cavern which has three other exits leading from it; one to your left, one to your right and the main one, carved as a giant skull, lying directly opposite. As you enter, an ugly robed man steps out of the mouth of the skull, holding a glass prism in his outstretched hands. He commands you to turn back as only the Snow Witch's personal servants are allowed inside the mountain. If you have a magic flute you may wish to tell him that you have been asked to come and play it for the Snow Witch (turn to **299**); or you may attack him with your sword (turn to **156**).

126

The Brain Slayer's disgusting tentacles flail frantically as it concentrates its mental power in an effort to draw you towards it. Unable to resist, you walk in a trance towards the hideous creature. You can only watch helplessly as it wraps one of its tentacles around your head. You feel weak and soon black out as the Brain Slayer begins to feed on your brainpower. Lose 2 *SKILL* points and 6 *STAMINA* points. If you are still alive, turn to **213**.

127

Once again your sword fails to find its mark and the dagger cuts into your sword arm. Lose 2 *STAMINA* points and 1 *SKILL* point. In desperation you hack frantically at the three images that lunge at you with daggers drawn. *Test your Luck*. If you are Lucky, turn to **232**. If you are Unlucky, turn to **361**.

128

You are able to walk silently past the sleeping Barbarian and continue up the gorge (turn to **319**).

129

You are knocked unconscious by the blow to your head. Already weakened by the Death Spell, the injury is more than you can withstand. Your adventure ends here.

130

You are now wearing a magic ring which has the power to summon a warrior to your aid once only. Add 1 *LUCK* point. If you have not already done so, you may either put on the gold ring (turn to **21**) or put on the silver ring (turn to **159**). Alternatively, you may walk through to the next tunnel (turn to **338**).

131

Further along the bank you find a small wooden boat tied to a tree. You look around but you cannot see its owner. If you wish to take the boat and row across the river, turn to **26**. If you would rather wait for its owner to arrive, turn to **289**.

132

The dagger just misses the knob, bouncing off the stone wall. If you have another dagger, turn to **16**. If you do not possess another dagger, turn to **393**.

133

You thrust out your hands and luckily manage to land on the floor without hurting yourself. As you pick yourself up, you suddenly hear footsteps coming from the depths of the cave. In the distance you can see a swaying light and the vague outline of a hunched, sinewy figure, who skulks slowly forward. If you wish to see who is coming towards you, turn to **37**. If you would rather run out of the cave, turn to **355**.

134

Your mind is completely controlled by the Snow Witch and you find yourself obeying her command. You drop the garlic and bare your neck in readiness for her to drink your blood. You will be her servant forever in the world of the undead.

135

The tunnel ends at another door, an old piece of parchment is pinned on it. There is faded writing on the parchment, but you do not understand the language. Knowing that elves speak many languages, you ask Redswift to try to read it. As he reads, his eyes widen with terror. You ask him what is wrong, but he refuses to reply. He rips the parchment off the door and tears it into tiny pieces. He turns the door handle and says, 'Let's get going, there is no time to lose.' You and Stubb look at each other and shrug your shoulders, deciding simply to obey the troubled Redswift. The door opens into another tunnel. After walking down it for a few metres, you come to a place where water is dripping down continuously from stalactites overhead. If you have a shield, turn to **230**. If you do not possess a shield, turn to **79**.

136

You soon arrive at the fork in the tunnel that the Mountain Elf mentioned and, deciding to take his advice, you enter the tunnel to your right (turn to **106**).

137

The tunnel ends quite soon at a T-junction. To your left you can hear cries for help. If you wish to turn left, turn to **311**. If you wish to turn right, turn to **125**.

138

The Snow Witch stares at you again before making her choice. This time she calls out 'Star!' Terror spreads across your face as you unfold your clenched fist, revealing the star-shaped metal disc. The Snow Witch laughs and another energy bolt shoots out of her globe. It slams into your chest, killing you instantly. Your adventure is over.

139

Intrigued by the open sarcophagus, you decide to walk over to examine it (turn to **297**).

140

The Goblins are well practised in the art of dagger-throwing and both hit you, one in the shoulder and one in the back of your thigh. Lose 4 *STAMINA* points and 1 *SKILL* point. You stop briefly to pull the daggers out and throw them back at the Goblins before running painfully on (turn to **29**).

141

A pouch on the Cave-man's belt contains a star-shaped metal disc which you decide to put in your backpack. Not wishing to meet any more Cave-men, you run along the tunnel to catch up with Redswift and Stubb (turn to **365**).

142

Ash is strong enough to keep hold of the rope bridge with one hand and to grab you with his other hand to stop you from being swept away downstream. He manages to drag you up on to the far bank, but the ordeal costs you 1 *STAMINA* point. Without waiting for you to recover, he urges you to follow him along the footpath which leads up the side of the hill away from the bridge (turn to **85**).

143

The followers are a group of Goblins, Orcs and Neanderthals. There are too many of them for you to overcome and you are soon captured. They drag you over to a circle of ice, dyed blue, in which the effigy stands. Amid wails and wild shouting, they throw you into the blue circle. The effigy immediately jerks its frozen limbs into motion – you have unleashed the power of an ICE DEMON.

ICE DEMON	*SKILL 9*	*STAMINA 11*

In addition to its normal attack, throw one die every Attack Round for the jet of freezing gas that shoots out from its nostrils. On a roll of 1, 2 or 3 the gas will hit you and reduce your *STAMINA* by 1 point, but on a roll of 4, 5 or 6 the gas will miss you. If you win, turn to **184**.

144

You ask the Centaurs if they saw any monsters during their gallop north across the Pagan Plain. Their leader looks at you sternly and says, 'No.' Seeing your wounds and bulging backpack, he asks if you have just returned from a treasure hunt. If you wish to reply that you have, turn to **272**. If you wish to reply that you were attacked by Dark Elves crossing the River Kok and your backpack contains merely their helmets and broken weapons, turn to **233**

145

You draw your sword and head down the tunnel. Two GOBLINS with ugly faces run into view, both wearing glowing metal collars round their necks. They see you and advance, snarling, with daggers drawn.

	SKILL	STAMINA
First GOBLIN	5	5
Second GOBLIN	5	4

Fight them one at a time in the narrow tunnel. If you win, turn to **347**.

146

The image of the bird fills your mind. While you are still asleep, you sit up and shout the word 'Phoenix' at the top of your voice. You wake up startled, wondering why it is dark. Then you realize that you have been asleep for hours and that the sun will rise at any moment. Adjusting your sun-mask, you turn to face east, hardly daring to blink in case you miss the first rays of sunshine. A red glow appears on the horizon and then you see the sun slowly creep up into view. You are cured of the Death Spell (turn to **400**).

147

Before the writing fades away, you learn a spell which will protect you against an attack by an Air Elemental. Add 1 *LUCK* point. You memorize the words 'Gul Sang Abi Daar'; and then decide what to do next. If you have not done so already, you may either look inside the red pot (turn to **101**) or leave the cavern by the door opposite (turn to **176**).

148

You step over the pieces of broken quartz that were once the Crystal Warrior, and carry on along the tunnel until it ends at a T-junction. If you wish to go left, turn to **150**. If you wish to go right, turn to **368**.

149

You open your backpack and reluctantly pay the man 50 Gold Pieces. Still smiling, he takes a jar from a shelf and pours the contents into a pan of soup which is simmering on an open fire in his kitchen. He fills a bowl with his herbal remedy and hands it to you, saying, 'That should do the job. It will take about an hour to work, so I suggest you go and lie down in the sun by the river. You'll soon be feeling much better.' You gulp down the soup, thank him curtly, and walk back down the footpath to find a spot to rest (turn to **209**).

150

The tunnel ends at a wooden door which opens when you turn the handle. You walk into a massive high-ceilinged chamber which ends in a wall of ice. In the centre of the chamber is an open marble sarcophagus with its lid propped up against its side. A white rat suddenly jumps out of the sarcophagus and runs towards you. It stops in front of you and starts to grow and change shape. If you possess any ground minotaur horn, turn to **52**. If you do not, turn to **223**.

151

You are too weak to keep your head above the surface. You are dragged under and breathe in some water. Lose 2 *STAMINA* points. If you still wish to keep your backpack on, turn to **360**. If you wish to take it off, turn to **42**.

152

The Snow Witch stares at you for a long time before calling out 'Circle.' You exhale loudly and unfold your clenched fist, revealing the circular metal disc. The Snow Witch is angry and tells you that the rules have changed. She now wins if the next result is a draw as well. You curse her, but you have to choose again. Will you:

Conceal the square disc?	Turn to **270**
Conceal the circular disc?	Turn to **291**
Conceal the star disc?	Turn to **138**

153

Your escape plan has failed and you are trapped inside the mountain tunnels. You know it will not be long before the Snow Witch's guards discover you and condemn you to a life of slavery. You have failed in your mission.

The dreaded Banshee comes into view

154

You suddenly hear a woman howling terribly in the depths of the cave. Her mournful wail rises to a horrible, bitter scream. The Healer whispers to you that the cries come from a BANSHEE, a hideous spectre whose face and hands are shrivelled and who only has one large nostril and a single tooth. He tells you that if you walk by her without fear, you will come to no harm. 'Do not speak to her, touch her or even acknowledge her presence. She cannot harm you if you obey my instructions. I will be right behind you, but do not worry about me,' the Healer says calmly. You walk further into the cave until the dreaded Banshee comes into view. She looks even worse than the Healer's description with her red-rimmed eyes and stooping posture. You try to remain calm but feel the blood racing through your veins. She stands immediately in front of you as you try to walk by, letting out the most doom-laden howl you have ever heard in your life. You are tempted to look into her face and cut her down with your sword. If you have drunk the dragon's egg concoction, turn to **5**. If you have not drunk this concoction, turn to **333**.

155

You look round and are relieved to see that Redswift and Stubb have both dispensed with their adversaries. You rummage quickly through the pouches on the Goblins' belts, but find only stale bread and charcoal sticks. However, if your sword is broken, you may take another one from the Goblins. Add 1 *SKILL* point. Despite the pain from your burns, you tell Redswift and Stubb that you are ready to move on. Leaning on Stubb, who always looks cheerful, you manage to hobble down the tunnel (turn to **166**).

156

The ugly man sneers as you draw your sword; he rubs the prism, and suddenly three identical images of himself appear. They walk towards you, each one has a dagger raised in his right hand. Two of the images must be illusions, but which will you strike with your sword? Will you:

Strike the man to your left?	Turn to **99**
Strike the man in the middle?	Turn to **307**
Strike the man to your right?	Turn to **232**

157

The shaft is icy and it slips from your grip as you release it. The spear misses the Yeti, plummeting harmlessly into the snow. Turn to **378**.

158

You breathe in and take a gulp of the green liquid. Feeling no ill effects, you quickly finish it off. Slowly the tiredness and pain in your body fade away and you feel revitalized. You have drunk a Potion of Health. Add 1 *SKILL* point, 4 *STAMINA* points and 1 *LUCK* point. Turn to **173**.

159

You are now wearing a ring which drains your life force. Roll one die and deduct the number from your *SKILL* score. Roll two dice and deduct the total from your *STAMINA* score. If you are still alive, you pull the cursed ring off your finger and crush it beneath your foot. If you have not done so already, you may either put on the gold ring (turn to **21**) or the copper ring (turn to **130**). Alternatively, you may walk through to the next tunnel (turn to **338**).

160

The force of the Elemental picks you up and slams you against the wall. Lose 1 *SKILL* point and 4 *STAMINA* points. If you have any dragon's eggs in your backpack, they are now broken and must be crossed off your *Equipment List*. If you are still alive, turn to **372**.

161

You finally reach the end of the gorge and wonder where to head next. The effect of the Death Spell is accelerating– lose 2 *STAMINA* points. You are beginning to lose hope of finding the Healer. If you wish to continue walking east over the edge of the gorge, turn to **302**. If you would rather walk back down the gorge, turn to **269**.

162

You nearly slip off a couple of the rocks, but manage to reach the far bank safely (turn to **50**).

163

You look up to see great cascades of snow tumbling down the mountain. Fortunately the avalanche sweeps down a ridge adjacent to the one you are climbing (turn to **363**).

164

You find a magnificent sword clenched in the hand of one of the dead Trolls. You unbend its fingers and take the finely crafted weapon. Its edge is keen and without any effort you slice through a nearby branch. Add 1 *SKILL* point. Redswift urges you to hurry in case there are more Trolls nearby (turn to **38**).

165

The key fits the lock and turns. Add 1 *LUCK* point. You continue down the tunnel, turning right, and soon arrive at a crossroads. There are no signs of life either from straight ahead or from the branch to your right, but advancing towards you along the left-hand branch is a strange humanoid (turn to **59**).

166

After walking for another five minutes, the tunnel turns sharply right and right again a few metres further on. You soon arrive at a junction and after a discussion you decide to turn left rather than continue straight on (turn to **259**).

167

The Rattlesnake bites you on the leg just above the rim of your boot. Before you can cut off its head it empties the poison from its fangs into your leg. Lose 4 *STAMINA* points. If you are still alive, you drain off the poison and limp up the gorge (turn to **252**).

168

The footpath twists and turns through the trees before ending outside a wooden hut. You creep up to the hut and look through the window. An old man wearing purple robes and a grey skull cap is asleep in an ornately carved rocking-chair. The shelves on the wall behind him are lined with jars of herbs and berries. If you wish to enter the hut, turn to **341**. If you would rather walk back down the path to continue up the valley, turn to **205**.

169

Underneath an overhanging rock, you see a small wooden hut built against the side of the mountain. Its roof is piled high with snow and long icicles hang down from the window ledges. You see a set of deep footprints leading from the hut up the side of the mountain. If you wish to enter the hut, turn to **36**. If you would rather follow the footprints in the snow, turn to **190**.

170

You scramble up the side of the gorge to reach the cave entrance. It is to0 dark to see inside and you do not have a lantern. If you wish to shout in the hope that the Healer lives there, turn to **53**. If you would rather just enter the cave, turn to **246**.

The guardian of the Snow Witch's treasure is dead and you are free to help yourself to her riches, although there is a limit to how much you can carry. You decide to fill your backpack with Gold Pieces, and you count 600 in all. However, for each 50 you take, you will have to remove one item from your backpack and leave it behind. Adjust your *Equipment List* accordingly. Just as you finish filling your backpack, you hear the sound of running feet coming down the tunnel towards the chamber. You stand up and draw your sword, wondering if you can survive much more hard combat. Two men suddenly appear at the door, a Dwarf and an Elf, but they do not look as though they are about to attack you. They are smiling broadly and they both try to speak at once, the Elf finally taking command. 'You have killed her! We are free! We will soon be able to take off our obedience collars! Now we wish to repay you, friend, by helping you to escape. You cannot leave the caverns by the way you came, because the Snow Witch's followers are waiting for you, and the tunnels are alive with Goblins. Our fellow Elves and Dwarfs are battling against them now, to give you time to flee – we must waste no more time.' To your surprise the Elf walks straight towards the cavern wall opposite the door, and appears to pass right through it. 'Another of the Snow Witch's illusions,' comments the Dwarf, 'an escape route she never got the chance to use. The trouble is, we've never used it either.' The Dwarf laughs to himself and walks towards the wall, you following behind. Walking through the illusion you find yourself in a narrow torchlit tunnel which you walk down in single file. It soon ends at a junction and you discuss which way to turn. If you wish to turn left, turn to **61**. If you would rather turn right, turn to **388**.

172

Ignoring a dark cave entrance at the foot of the mountain, you begin the difficult climb up the steep face. You suddenly slip and fall when a piece of rock comes away in your hand. *Test your Luck*. If you are Lucky, turn to **284**. If you are Unlucky, you will plunge to your death down the side of Firetop Mountain.

173

It is not long before Stubb returns, laden with nuts, roots, greens and a fat rabbit. Using a pan he found in the bottom of the boat, he sets about making a delicious stew, while Redswift brags about his fight with the Dark Elf. Soon you are all enjoying the nourishing meal, telling each other stories and putting the terrible memories of the Snow Witch out of your minds. Add 4 *STAMINA* points. Later you climb into the Dark Elf's boat and push off from the bank. It does not take long to reach the other side and you set off south across the Pagan Plain for Stonebridge (turn to **278**).

174

You are tempted to turn round and walk back to Big Jim Sun's caravan – but your reputation is at stake, and you have no choice but to carry on with the grim trek up the mountainside (turn to **169**).

175

Ash fires a perfect shot: his arrow pierces the head of the diving Death Hawk. Its wings stop beating and it crashes into the side of the hill. The other side of the hill slopes down into a gorge and Ash tells you that you must now journey alone to meet the Healer. He tells you to walk east up the gorge until you see the head of a phoenix carved in the rock. The Healer lives in a cave in the side of the hill above the carved rock. You thank Ash for his help and walk slowly down the hill into the gorge. At the bottom you follow Ash's instructions and turn left up the gorge (turn to **252**).

176

The door opens into yet another tunnel and you begin to wonder whether you will ever find your way out of the caverns of the Snow Witch. You look at Redswift and Stubb, but they do not appear to be very concerned. The tunnel soon ends at another door and you notice a dagger sticking out of its oak panelling. If you wish to pull the dagger out of the door, turn to **55**. If you would rather open the door, turn to **285**.

Each one is armed with a bow and quiver of arrows

177

Pulling the dart from your arm, you flee from the followers and run into the tunnel (turn to **137**).

178

You fall to the ground, hitting your head on a rock. If you are wearing a helmet, turn to **324**. If you are not wearing a helmet, turn to **129**.

179

The Gnome does not want to end up like the Neanderthal and runs out of the cave shouting for help. If you wish to search through the cupboards and risk the Gnome returning with reinforcements, turn to **194**. If you would rather leave the cave immediately, turning left into the tunnel, turn to **198**.

180

The thundering noise of galloping hooves grows louder and four CENTAURS come into view. Each one is armed with a bow and quiver of arrows. They stop almost at once in a line before you, keen-eyed and ready for any move on your part. Their leader is obviously the one with the ugly blue scar running down his face and chest, as he is also proudly carrying a spear and a shield, and wearing a horned helmet. If you wish to offer to pay them to take you to Stonebridge, turn to **329**. If you would rather just talk to them briefly and be on your way, turn to **144**.

181

Before you can scramble on to the far bank, the bridge collapses under you and crashes into the river. *Test your Luck*. If you are Lucky, turn to **142**. If you are Unlucky, turn to **277**.

182

You walk over to the broken chest and examine its contents: three ornate rings and a cracked bottle which emits a sweet odour. If you wish to try on any of the rings, turn to **65**. If you would rather walk through to the next tunnel, turn to **338**.

183

As soon as you touch the shield, a howling wind starts to blow down the tunnel towards you, almost knocking the three of you off your feet. Then you see a whirlwind coming down the tunnel, gathering up all rocks and stones in its path. If the words 'Gul Sang Abi Daar' mean anything to you, turn to **253**. If they mean nothing to you, turn to **66**.

184

The Ice Demon crashes to the floor in a pile of broken ice. The Snow Witch's followers fall back in terror, afraid that you might now possess the Demon's powers. Add 1 *LUCK* point. Unchallenged, you are able to leave the cave by the tunnel exit (turn to **137**).

185

Between her screams the Banshee tells you that you are going to die. You are unable to resist the temptation to draw your sword and silence her.

BANSHEE   *SKILL 12*   *STAMINA 12*

Before each Attack Round, you must roll two dice. If the total is the same or less than your *SKILL*, you will not be paralysed by fear and you will be able to fight. If the total is greater than your *SKILL* score, you will automatically lose that Attack Round. If you win, turn to **19**.

186

The energy bolt which hits you gives your system a terrible shock. You are knocked to the ground by its force. Lose 1 *SKILL* point and 4 *STAMINA* points. If you are still alive, turn to **98**.

187

As you draw your sword, the. Gnome yells an order to the dull-witted NEANDERTHAL, telling him to kill you. The Neanderthal grunts and stands up, pushing the table away from him. He picks up a carving knife and a stool as a shield and lumbers forward to attack.

NEANDERTHAL   SKILL 7   STAMINA 8

If you win, turn to **179**.

188

Neither of the Goblins releases the rope and both tumble headlong into the pit. Only one of the two picks himself up, the other remaining face down on the ice floor. With blood streaming from his nose, the angry Goblin pulls a dagger from his belt and tries to stab you. In the confined space of the pit, you must defend yourself with your bare hands.

GOBLIN   *SKILL 5*   *STAMINA 4*

During each round of combat, you must reduce your Attack Strength by 3 as you are without your sword. If you win, turn to **366**.

189

The Brain Slayer's disgusting tentacles flail frantically as it tries to draw you towards it. Fortunately the amulet gives you the courage to resist its attempt to hypnotize you. You draw your sword to attack the foul creature. It releases Redswift and Stubb who fall to the floor clutching their heads in agony.

BRAIN SLAYER   *SKILL 10*   *STAMINA 10*

If you win, turn to **309**.

It is the killer beast that you have been hunting

190

The high altitude and thin atmosphere make you pant for breath as you continue your steady climb. Lose 1 *STAMINA* point. Suddenly you hear the cry of a human voice followed by a ferocious roar. Not far ahead you see a fur trapper fighting for his life against a gigantic bear-like beast with long white fur and sharp teeth protruding from its jaws. It is the killer beast that you have been hunting – the abominable YETI. You watch the unfortunate trapper being gashed by the Yeti's claws and falling face down in the snow. Incensed by the vicious attack you scream at the Yeti and run through the snow to attack it (turn to **77**).

191

You are so weak that the effort of trying to haul yourself up the vine is too much for you. You lose your grip and fall headlong ten metres down on to the dirt floor and land on a pile of bones. Unable to move and semi-conscious, you feel helpless as hundreds of Flesh Grubs crawl on to you to begin their feast. Your adventure ends here.

192

As you are about to leave the hut, you catch sight of some weapons lying under the bed. If you wish to take a couple of them with you, turn to **255**. If you do not wish to be encumbered by the additional weight and would rather leave without the weapons, turn to **263**.

193

You quickly dive on to the floor and watch the energy bolt pass overhead and slam into the cavern wall behind you (turn to **336**).

194

The cupboards are full of pots, pans, bowls and spoons. One cupboard is locked and you have to prise it open with your sword. It contains the Gnome's personal possessions – a silver flute, a rune-carved wooden stick painted with blue and yellow hoops, an old withered rose and an old leather-bound book entitled 'The Secrets of Toads'. Will you:

Blow the flute?	Turn to **74**
Read the runes on the stick?	Turn to **345**
Smell the rose?	Turn to **317**
Read the book?	Turn to **356**
Leave the possessions and turn left back into the tunnel?	Turn to **198**

195

Your hand is too numb and painful for you to grip the spear. You curse and hurl it into the snow, drawing your sword with your other hand to fight the huge white beast.

YETI   *SKILL* 11   *STAMINA* 12

If you win, turn to **67**.

196

Stubb draws the short straw and reaches for the handle, cursing his luck. As soon as he touches it, it comes alive. An ASP curls itself around his hand, and before he can shake it off, it sinks its poisonous fangs into his wrist. He falls on to his knees clutching his wrist with his other hand. Redswift quickly draws off the poison with his knife: luckily the Dwarf has a strong constitution, and he soon recovers enough strength to continue (turn to **20**).

197

You fall headlong down the crevasse, landing heavily on an icy ledge some ten metres below. Roll 1 die. Deduct this number from your current *STAMINA* score. Using your sword, you cut hand- and toe-holds into the side of the crevasse and haul yourself up. Plodding your way through the thick snow, you continue your quest (turn to **212**).

198

In the distance you hear chanting voices; before long the tunnel ends at the entrance to a large cavern. Kneeling down before an ice effigy in the shape of a demon, their hooded faces pressed to the ice floor in worship, are ten of the Snow Witch's followers. There are two exits from the cave, one to your left and one to your right. If you are wearing a cloak, turn to **384**. If you are not wearing a cloak, turn to **260**.

199

After the ordeal with the Werewolf you cannot settle down to sleep again. You are pleased when Stubb completes the second watch and asks you to take over. The rest of the night passes peacefully and in the morning you are able to continue your journey to Stonebridge (turn to **13**).

200

The Zombie was probably in charge of the storeroom that the door opens into. Jars and bottles of various shapes and sizes line the walls and many boxes and barrels are stacked up on the floor. You search quickly through them and find little of interest except for a jar of ground minotaur horn, some garlic, a box full of teeth, a jar of pickled lizards' tails and four large dragon eggs. As you will not be able to fit everything into your backpack, you may only take three of the items. Leaving the room, you walk back to the junction and head straight on down the tunnel (turn to **150**).

201

You see an overhanging branch and just manage to grab it with one hand. If you are carrying a shield, you will have to let it drop into the river (lose 1 *SKILL* point) so that you can haul yourself out. Summoning all your remaining strength, you manage to pull yourself up on to the south bank of the river. You feel totally exhausted. Lose 2 *STAMINA* points. You curse the Snow Witch and set off east, back towards the place where the fire was burning (turn to **50**).

202

You step past the still bodies of the Wolves and continue your journey through the swirling snow. The climb becomes steeper and the going is slow. Turn to **337**.

203

Stubb draws the short straw and chuckles with pleasure. He kicks off his old boots and eagerly puts on the magical elfin boots. To test them out, he jumps up and down on the stone floor, and makes no noise when he lands. Impatient to walk in his new boots, he heads off along the tunnel with you and Redswift following (turn to **20**).

204

The Elf slumps on to the floor and pulls back his hood. You see a metal collar around his neck, glowing in the semi-darkness. 'Obedience collar,' he stammers in pain. 'Makes us do whatever she wishes. If I die it will lose its energy but she will know and send others to investigate. Elves, even we Mountain Elves, would not serve that vile witch of our own free will. Kill her and free us. I bear you no grudge for attacking me, for you knew no better. Take my cloak to disguise yourself and follow this tunnel to where it branches. Take the right-hand fork. Now I must rest.' You put the Elf's cloak round your shoulders and make him as comfortable as you can. You shake his hand and run off down the tunnel (turn to **136**).

205

You spot a small open space between the rocks and trees on the far bank of the river. Something is cooking over a fire, you can see the smoke rising; but there is no one to be seen – perhaps they saw you first and are hiding. The river runs fast and is quite narrow at this point. Large rocks jut out of the river and it would be possible to cross over by leaping from rock to rock. If you wish to cross, turn to **268**. If you would rather keep on walking up the river valley, turn to **115**.

206

The Healer looks concerned and says, Then you have no alternative, you must walk to Firetop Mountain and climb it alone. This is where we say goodbye. Good luck, I hope you make it.' You shake the Healer's hand, thanking him for his help. Then, waving goodbye, you squeeze through the crack into the daylight. Knowing that the effect of the Death Spell has been temporarily halted, you journey north at a fast pace. You are quite close to the foot of the mountain when an ugly creature jumps out from behind a rock to challenge you. It is a HOBGOBLIN and you must fight it.

HOBGOBLIN   *SKILL* 6   *STAMINA* 7

If you win, turn to **172**.

207

The tunnel soon turns sharply left. As you turn the corner you see something on the floor, sparkling in the dim light. You bend down and pick up a circular metal disc. Hoping that it might be useful, you put it in your pocket. It's not long before the tunnel turns sharply left again and you soon arrive at a junction. After some discussion, you decide to turn right rather than continue straight on (turn to **259**).

208

As the Mountain Elf slumps on to the floor, his strange metal collar stops glowing. You wonder what is happening and decide to hurry down the tunnel (turn to **241**).

209

Feeling ill, you lie down in the sun and soon fall asleep. You wake up an hour later but you do not feel any better – in fact, you feel worse. You realize that the man who sold you the herbs was not the Healer, but an opportunist sham. The hour you have wasted waiting for the fake remedy to work has cost you dearly. Lose 3 *STAMINA* points. If you wish to go back to the herbalist's hut, turn to **27**. If you would rather not waste any more time and continue up the river valley, turn to **205**.

210

The Snow Witch recoils from the garlic, giving you time to think. You know that a Vampire can only be killed by driving a stake through its heart. If you possess a carved rune stick, turn to **34**. If not, turn to **10**.

211

Stubb's desire for revenge spurs him on and he quickly defeats two of the Hill Trolls, and then helps Redswift dispatch the remaining two. He does not stop to search through the Trolls' belongings, but heads straight for

Stonebridge. You follow him into the village where he is greeted by all his old friends. However, you soon discover that an air of gloom hangs over the Dwarfs. Even though they know that the Hill Trolls are gathering to attack their village, they have lost their will to defend themselves since their fabled war-hammer was stolen from King Gillibran. Stubb is concerned by their loss of morale and takes you to the inn to meet his friend Bigleg. He learns from Bigleg that an eagle took the war-hammer but dropped it over Darkwood Forest. 'Then we must find it. Bigleg, we must leave immediately,' says Stubb, forgetting his own troubles. He stands up and extends his hand to you, saying, 'Well, friends, I'm sorry, but I will not be able to offer you our hospitality after all. I hope you understand.' He walks out of the inn with Bigleg and that is the last that you see of the jolly old Dwarf. Redswift sighs and suggests that the two of you leave for Moonstone Hills straight away. Besides, he says, he has something important to tell you and in a way it is fortunate that Stubb will not be around to hear what he has to say. Intrigued by Redswift's words, you leave Stonebridge, heading east along the bank of Red River. While keeping a lookout for Hill Troll patrols, you cannot help wondering what it is that Redswift has to tell you. Hidden among the trees to your left, Redswift suddenly spots three Hill Trolls sharpening their weapons on a stone. *Test your Luck*, If you are Lucky, turn to **218**. If you are Unlucky, turn to **296**.

Suddenly one leaps at you

212

The wind starts to howl, blowing gusts of snow into your face. You put your head down and stride into it. Above the howl of the wind you suddenly become aware of another sound – the howling of wolves. You draw your sword while trying to peer through the snow. As if out of nowhere, two SNOW WOLVES appear in front of you, hunched ready to pounce. They are completely white except for their blood-red eyes. Suddenly one leaps at you. Fight them one at a time.

	SKILL	STAMINA
First SNOW WOLF	7	8
Second SNOW WOLF	7	7

If you win, turn to **202**.

213

You wake to find Redswift and Stubb lying unconscious on the floor. There is no sign of the Brain Slayer. You groan as you try to sit up, the pain in your head is almost unbearable. Your two companions eventually come round, they are obviously suffering too. They explain that the Brain Slayer drew them into the cavern and they were powerless to resist. You examine the chamber and see another door opposite in the far wall. There are also two clay pots in a recess in the wall, one red and one grey.

Will you:

Open the door?	Turn to **176**
Look inside the red pot?	Turn to **101**
Look inside the grey pot?	Turn to **344**

214

As soon as you step into the tunnel, an iron grille drops down behind you, barring your retreat. The man laughs out loud and says, 'You were foolish to think you could trick me so easily when all the world can see you are not wearing your obedience collar. Now, intruder, you are trapped.' There is nothing you can do but find out what lies at the end of the tunnel (turn to **323**).

215

The tunnel opens out into a small cavern which is empty apart from a brass bowl resting on top of an ice plinth. The bowl contains a yellow liquid and a wooden ladle. If you wish to drink some of the liquid, turn to **24**. If you would rather walk back out of the cavern without drinking the liquid, turn to **56**.

216

You quickly load your sling and aim at the globe. Roll two dice. If the total is the same or less than your *SKILL*, turn to **282**. If the total is greater than your *SKILL*, turn to **375**.

217

The red leaves all around you emit a sweet smell which you find very pleasant. You feel very relaxed and suddenly have trouble keeping your eyes open, even though it is only early evening. You are unaware that you are lying on SLEEPING GRASS. You sink into a deep sleep, full of vivid and exciting dreams. Night falls and time passes by, but you cannot wake up. The moon drifts slowly across the clear night sky until dawn is only minutes away. A tiny image disturbs your dreams but it is difficult to make out; it grows steadily larger, until the flashing image fills your mind. A bird with a long beak and fine plumage is trying to fly out of a circle of flames. The Healer is trying to wake you. If you can focus your mind and remember the name of this bird, which is the symbol of the Healer's power, your dreams will end and you will be able to rouse yourself. If you believe the bird to be a Phoenix, turn to **146**. If you believe the bird to be a Griffin, turn to **228**.

218

The Hill Trolls do not see you and you are able to slip by them unnoticed (turn to **38**).

219

The spear flies through the air and thuds into the Yeti's shaggy chest. It roars in pain but does not fall. You quickly draw your sword to fight the enraged beast.

YETI   *SKILL* 10   *STAMINA* 9

If you win, turn to **67**.

220

Stepping carefully between the footprints, you expect something sinister to happen at any moment. However, nothing happens until Stubb sneezes loudly and startles you. Roll 1 die. If you roll a 1 or 2, turn to **94**. If you roll a 3 or 4, turn to **326**. If you roll a 5 or 6, turn to **107**.

221

The tunnel turns sharply to the right at the entrance to another cave, from which you can hear a stringed instrument playing gentle music. Your view into the cave is partially blocked by an old tattered animal skin hanging down over the entrance, but you can see the lower torso of a man wearing green and purple hose and pointed red slippers. If you wish to throw back the animal skin and enter the cave, turn to **303**. If you would rather keep walking along the tunnel, turn to **111**.

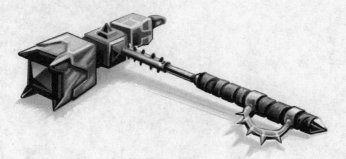

222

You manage to haul yourself out of the hollow tree, but some Flesh Grubs are clinging to your body. Roll 1 die to determine how many are buried in your flesh and deduct 1 *STAMINA* point for each. If you are still alive, turn to **242**.

Before you stands an ancient White Dragon

223

The creature soon towers above you and develops a rough white reptilian skin. Its neck extends to support a giant head with smoking nostrils, and wings protrude from its back. Before you stands an ancient WHITE DRAGON. If you are wearing a copper ring, turn to **313**. If not, you must fight the mighty beast as you stand.

WHITE DRAGON   *SKILL 12*   *STAMINA 14*

In addition to its normal attack, throw one die every attack round for its freezing cold breath. Unless you are wearing a gold ring, a roll of 1 or 2 will reduce your *STAMINA* score by a further 2 points. A roll of 3-6 will mean the icy blast misses you. If you win, turn to **139**.

224

As soon as you begin reading the scroll, the writing starts to fade. Roll two dice. If the total is the same or less than your *SKILL*, turn to **147**. If the total is greater than your *SKILL*, turn to **396**.

225

The blizzard has affected you badly. Your sword-hand is frostbitten and you are very weak. You will now have to use your other arm to fight. Lose 3 *SKILL* points and 4 *STAMINA* points. If you are still alive, turn to **174**.

226

Both the dart and the whip fail to find their mark and you are able to run through the tunnel (turn to **137**).

227

The Dark Elf is an excellent shot. The arrow thuds into your shoulder and you let out a painful cry. Lose 2 *STAMINA* points. Stubb quickly takes hold of the oars and continues to row the boat towards the far bank. However, you are still within the range of the Dark Elf's arrows. You watch him pick another arrow and fire again. *Test your Luck*. If you are Lucky, turn to **32**, if you are Unlucky, turn to **239**.

228

The image of the bird starts to fade as vivid dreams fill your mind again. You have failed to recognize the fabled bird that the Healer so admires, and he no longer thinks you are worthy of his help. When dawn breaks you are still fast asleep, your opportunity to break the Death Spell has gone. It is the beginning of a beautiful day, but one that you will never see. Firetop Mountain has provided more food for its hungry vultures.

229

The temperature is well below freezing point and the howling blizzard chills you to the bone. You struggle to walk through the snowstorm, but it drains your energy. Lose 2 *STAMINA* points. If you still wish to walk through the blizzard, turn to **387**. If you would rather dig yourself a shelter in the snow with your sword, turn to **281**.

230

The water looks harmless enough, but you do not wish to get cold and wet. You place the shield over your head and walk under the gentle waterfall. You throw the shield back for your companions to use, and you are soon on your way again (turn to **339**).

231

By the time you reach the top of the hill, you are panting heavily. Lose 1 *STAMINA* point. Feeling exhausted, you stand and look around you. The hill slopes down into a gorge which runs east to west. You walk slowly down the hill into the gorge and turn left. After walking for a while, you see the entrance to a cave half-way up the left-hand side of the gorge. If you wish to climb up to the cave, turn to **170**. If you would rather keep on walking up the gorge, turn to **377**.

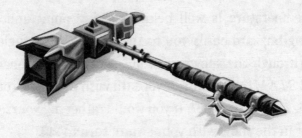

232

The Illusionist screams in pain as your sword cuts into his side. He drops to the floor as his other two images fade away. As you step over him, he starts to laugh and stands up, his wound completely healed. If you wish to thrust your sword at him again, turn to **261**. If you wish to try to smash his prism, turn to **72**.

233

The leader slowly nods his head. He believes your story and signals to the group to move on. You watch them gallop away, and, relieved at their departure, you march off together towards Stonebridge (turn to **278**).

234

You aim carefully between the iron bars and throw your dagger at the wooden knob. *Test your Luck*. If you are Lucky, turn to **120**. If you are Unlucky, turn to **132**.

*Suddenly it bursts out of your hands and
changes into a golden warrior*

235

You see frozen into the ice wall an ornate trunk open and filled with gold and jewels. You hack away at the ice until you reach the trunk. A golden idol is the first thing you pick up, but suddenly it bursts out of your hands and changes into a golden warrior – a SENTINEL left to guard the treasure.

SENTINEL   *SKILL 9*   *STAMINA 9*

If you win, turn to **171**.

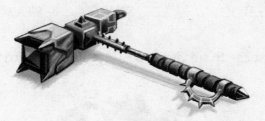

236

Despite straining with all their might, your friends are unable to force your hand against the door. The dagger's power makes your hand turn again and this time you plunge the blade into your side. Lose 1 *SKILL* point and 4 *STAMINA* points. If you are still alive, your friends try again to force the dagger into the door. *Test your Luck,* if you are Lucky, turn to **6** If you are Unlucky, turn to **35**.

237

Gripping the hilt firmly, you tug hard at the sword. It comes free with surprising ease. You have chosen the Sword of Speed, an almost weightless yet strong and sharp sword. Add 1 *SKILL* point. If you wish to rummage through the Orc's backpack, turn to **354**. If you wish to walk directly through to the tunnel opposite, turn to **221**.

238

Ash's arrow just misses the diving Death Hawk. Before he is able to fire again, the Death Hawk attacks you.

DEATH HAWK   *SKILL 4*   *STAMINA 5*

If you manage to survive two Attack Rounds, turn to **105**.

239

Even at long range the Dark Elf is an accurate bowman. His arrow sinks painfully into your thigh. Lose 2 *STAMINA* points. With Stubb rowing furiously, you at last reach the far bank before the Dark Elf has time to fire again. You jump out of the boat, gesture at the Dark Elf and set off south across the Pagan Plain towards Stonebridge (turn to **278**).

240

You just manage to jump out of the way of the plunging dagger. You stand, feet apart, ready to fight the enraged Goblin with your bare hands.

GOBLIN   *SKILL 5*   *STAMINA 5*

During each round of combat you must reduce your Attack Strength by 3, because you are without your sword. If you win, turn to **43**.

241

The tunnel forks and you must decide quickly which way to go. You can hear the sound of running feet coming down the branch to your right. If you wish to run down the left branch, turn to **321**. If you would rather head down the right branch to face whoever is coming towards you, turn to **145**.

242

You pull the hideous Grubs out of your flesh and crush them underfoot. Realizing that the Healer obviously does not live in the hollow tree, you continue to walk up the river valley (turn to **119**).

243

You wait until the Frost Giant has his back to you and then run through his lair. You reach the next tunnel before the slow-moving Giant realizes what is happening, but you do not stop running (turn to **338**).

244

Just before your sword hits the globe, a bolt of white light shoots out, trapping your blade. A searing pain rushes up your arm and the image of the Snow Witch laughs at your unsuccessful attempt to defeat her. You are unable to release your grip on the handle, and drop to your knees as the intensity of the charge increases. You black out and do not wake again. Your adventure ends here.

245

Both the daggers miss you, flying past on either side of your head. Add 1 *LUCK* point. You run on without stopping to look back (turn to **29**).

246

Inside the cave it is so dark that you can hardly see your hand in front of your face. As you walk on blindly, you stumble and trip. *Test your Luck*. If you are Lucky, turn to **133**. If you are Unlucky, turn to **178**.

247

You break the loaf in two and, to your surprise, find an iron key in its centre. Add 1 *LUCK* point. You put the key in your pocket, change your mind about eating the loaf and walk into the tunnel opposite (turn to **221**).

248

You regain consciousness to find Redswift and Stubb attending to your burns. 'I don't like to say I told you so,' Redswift says sarcastically. You try to walk but the pain is too severe. 'We'll have to rest here,' says Stubb, looking concerned, 'but it won't be long before the Snow Witch's Goblins find us.' There is nothing you can do but lie down again. *Test your Luck*. If you are Lucky, turn to **28**. If you are Unlucky, turn to **332**.

249

Gripping the shaft tightly, you pull back your arm and hurl the spear at the snarling Yeti. Roll one die. If you roll a 1, turn to **157**. If you roll a 2 or greater, turn to **219**.

250

Gripping the shaft of the spear firmly in your hands, you tug as hard as you can. The spear does not come free and your mind becomes filled with horrific images, making you scream out in terror. You release the spear; but the images remain, affecting your mind. Lose 1 *SKILL* point. If you wish to rummage through the Orc's backpack, turn to **354**. If you wish to walk directly through to the tunnel opposite, turn to **221**.

251

You have been asleep for only two hours when an eerie howl pierces the night air, waking you up. You see Redswift immediately stoke up the fire and Stubb run to his side, ready for battle. Suddenly you hear a twig snap behind you and you turn round to see a large beast about to leap on you. Its long hair and sharp teeth glisten in the firelight, and you realize it is a WEREWOLF. You must fight it.

WEREWOLF   *SKILL* 8   *STAMINA* 10

If you win, turn to **199**.

252

You see a rope-ladder hanging down from one of the trees on the left side of the gorge. Looking up, you can just make out the frame of a wooden hut, almost hidden among the branches. If you wish to climb up the ladder to the tree-house, turn to **398**. If you would rather continue up the gorge, turn to **92**.

253

Taking the shield has unleashed the fury of an AIR ELEMENTAL. Fortunately you remember the words on the scroll and utter them as the Elemental draws near. It disappears as quickly as it appeared, and all is calm again. You sling the shield on to your arm (add 1 *SKILL* point) and walk together back down the tunnel and past the last junction (turn to **135**).

254

You groan with pain and try to stand up. Looking up to see how far you have fallen, you are dismayed to see two ugly faces staring down at you. A rope is thrown down to you and you are ordered to throw your sword up to the GOBLINS before climbing up the rope. You are trapped in the pit and reluctantly comply with their orders. As you are about to climb, you notice that both the Goblins are holding the rope. If you wish to climb up, turn to **276**. If you wish to pull hard on the rope in an attempt to pull them down into the pit, turn to **314**.

255

You take a war-hammer and a spear before leaving the hut (turn to **263**).

256

You just manage to draw your sword in time to defend yourself against the diving Bird-man. It veers away slightly but turns to attack again.

BIRD-MAN   *SKILL 12*   *STAMINA 8*

If you win, turn to **18**.

257

You roll down the mountain but the avalanche soon runs out of momentum in a gully. Luckily, you are not buried in the snow and find yourself dazed but able to sit up. Lose 1 *SKILL* point. Still feeling dizzy, you stand up and start your climb again (turn to **363**).

258

The Healer walks over to you and puts his hands on your forehead. He mutters some strange words and stands back, saying, 'Later stages of the reversal process are also dangerous, but the danger can be reduced if you possess certain things. My help from now on will be limited as you will have to journey to another place to break the Death Spell completely. Please follow me.' The Healer walks further into the cave leading you to the edge of a pit. There is almost no light and you have to strain your eyes to see the outline of the Healer moving about. 'A log spans the pit before you and you must cross it to reach the inner cave. It will obviously be easier to cross it if you can see where you are going. Do you have a candle?' asks the Healer. If you possess a candle and tinder-box, turn to **54**. If you do not possess these items, turn to **343**.

259

Placed against the left-hand wall of the tunnel, you see a large iron casket with a brass handle in the shape of a serpent. No one volunteers to open the casket, so you decide to draw lots. Roll 1 die. If you roll a 1 or 2, turn to **73**. If you roll a 3 or 4, turn to **196**. If you roll a 5 or 6, turn to **353**.

260

You breathe in deeply and walk casually through the cavern towards the tunnel to your right (turn to **370**).

261

The Illusionist makes no attempt to block your sword as it cuts down through the air. Your sword, instead of striking the Illusionist, hits an invisible barrier and shatters, leaving you with the hilt and a short broken blade. Lose 1 *LUCK* point and 1 *SKILL* point. There is nothing you can do except try to grab his probable source of power – the prism. Turn to **72**.

262

As you try to stand up, the Snow Witch concentrates her powers on Redswift and Stubb. Their metal collars tighten and they both clutch their throats as if gasping for breath. You struggle to your feet, yelling insults at the Snow Witch, mocking her cowardly way of dealing with defenceless slaves. You challenge her to a combat, of whatever type she wishes. She laughs, saying, 'Even though I have beaten you, I enjoy games. I will play!' She releases her stranglehold on Redswift and Stubb and falls silent, obviously devising some fiendish contest. Suddenly you hear the sound of shuffling footsteps coming from the tunnel opposite. An Elf and a Dwarf enter the cavern: they look almost identical to Redswift and Stubb except that their vacant looks and putrid white flesh indicate that they are both ZOMBIES. The Snow Witch tells you to fight them while she invents a game for you to play. The Zombies lumber forward and you are forced to fight the terrible replicas of your friends.

	SKILL	STAMINA
DWARF ZOMBIE	8	9
ELF ZOMBIE	9	9

Fight both the Zombies at the same time. Each will have a separate attack on you during each Attack Round, but you must choose which of the two you will fight. Attack your nominated target as in a normal battle. Against the other, you will throw for your Attack Strength in the normal way, but you will not wound it if your Attack Strength is greater; you must count this as though you have just parried its blow. Of course, if its Attack Strength is greater, it will have wounded you in the normal way. If you win, turn to **23**.

263

Outside again in the deep snow, you set off on your trek up the mountainside, following the footprints in the snow (turn to **190**).

264

The Mountain Elf looks at you and smiles. 'Now you're talking,' he says. 'Kill her and free us. Here, take my cloak to disguise yourself and follow this tunnel until it branches. Take the right-hand fork. Good luck.' You shake the Elf's hand and run off down the tunnel (turn to **136**).

265

Redswift draws the short straw and smiles. He kicks off his old boots and puts on the magical elfin boots. He strides off down the corridor making not the slightest sound. You and Stubb are forced to follow him, feeling more than a little jealous (turn to **20**).

266

As soon as you step into the tunnel, an iron grille drops down behind you, barring your retreat. It is impossible to lift and there is nothing you can do but find out what lies at the end of the tunnel (turn to **323**).

267

You wait until the Gnome and the Neanderthal look away, before running past the cave opening and on down the tunnel (turn to **198**).

268

The rocks are slippery and far apart. In your present condition, you find it difficult to jump from rock to rock. Roll 1 die. If you roll a 1, 2 or 3, turn to **124**. If you roll a 4, 5 or 6, turn to **162**.

269

You soon arrive back at the carved rock slab and decide to climb up the stone steps that lead to the cave (turn to **75**).

270

The Snow Witch stares at you again before making her choice. This time she calls out 'Star.' Terror spreads across your face as you unfold your clenched fist, revealing the square metal disc. The Snow Witch laughs and another energy bolt shoots out from her globe. It slams into your chest, killing you instantly. Your adventure is over.

271

The Healer shakes his head and warns you that the next stage is going to be very difficult for you. He then tells you to walk ahead of him (turn to **154**).

272

The Centaur suddenly rears and charges forward, thrusting his spear at you. The other Centaurs follow his lead and charge at Redswift and Stubb. You have to react quickly to defend yourself against the Centaur bandit.

CENTAUR	SKILL 10	STAMINA 10

If you win, turn to **76**.

273

You just manage to scramble up on to the far bank as the bridge crashes down into the river. Ash urges you to follow him as quickly as possible along the footpath which leads up the side of the hill away from the bridge (turn to **85**).

274

The Mountain Elf looks at you in disbelief and says, 'Nobody of good heart would wish to join the Snow Witch. I am only here because of this!' Throwing back his hood, the Elf reveals a metal collar around his neck which glows in the semi-darkness. 'Only the obedience collar makes me serve her,' he continues in a dour voice. If you wish to reiterate your desire to join the Snow Witch, turn to **22**. If you would rather change your story and tell the Elf that you intend to slay her, turn to **264**.

275

Determined to discover the secret of the orb, you hold it in your outstretched hands. Its warmth starts to creep up your arms and soon you are glowing all over, and feeling warmer than you have been for weeks. Add 3 *STAMINA* points and 1 *LUCK* point. You assure Redswift and Stubb that this orb of energy will warm them too and they nervously pass it between them. In good spirits, you place the orb back on the floor and continue down the tunnel (turn to **166**).

276

You take hold of the rope and haul yourself out of the ice pit. The Goblins are dressed in furs and are wearing glowing metal collars around their necks. They motion you to walk back down the tunnel, urging you on with the points of their daggers. You realize that you are doomed unless you try to escape. If you wish to fight them with your bare hands, turn to **39**. If you would rather try to run away, turn to **102**.

277

Ash is strong enough to keep hold of the rope bridge, but he cannot reach you. You are thrown into the water and swept away downstream. You are too weak to survive the white-water rapids, and your adventure ends here.

278

Marching quickly across the plain you do not encounter any evil creatures. To the east, you see the forbidding shape of Firetop Mountain reaching into the sky. 'Does the Warlock still rule the depths of Firetop Mountain?' Stubb asks inquisitively. You are just about to reply when you see somebody walking towards you. You draw your sword, but when the person gets closer, you see that it is a little old man carrying a sack over his shoulder. He stops in front of you and says, 'Put that sword away, there's no point in killing me. The only thing I have to offer is information – and that costs money. Pay me 2 Gold Pieces and you won't regret it.' If you wish to pay the old man for his information, turn to **69**. If you would rather ignore him and continue south, turn to **348**.

279

The Illusionist withdraws his dagger and his three images prepare to strike you again. You decide to swipe your blade across all of the images in an attempt to strike the real Illusionist. *Test your Luck*. If you are Lucky, turn to **232**. If you are Unlucky, turn to **127**.

280

You see an overhanging branch, but just fail to grab it. You are carried further down the river before being pushed into an inlet where you come to a welcome halt. If you were carrying a shield, you would have lost it (lose 1 *SKILL* point). You have swallowed lots of water and are completely exhausted; you just have enough strength to clamber out of the river on to the south bank. Lose 4 *STAMINA* points. You curse your bad luck and set off east, back towards the place where the fire was burning (turn to **50**).

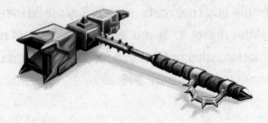

281

You hurriedly cut blocks of ice out of the mountainside and build a makeshift igloo. You crawl into it as the blizzard blows down the mountain with ferocious power. Your body-heat is retained inside the igloo and you keep warm. However, you must eat two portions of your Provisions to regain your strength after the tiring walk and the effort of building the igloo (this does not increase your *STAMINA*). An hour later, the blizzard dies down and you crawl out of your shelter to continue your quest (turn to **169**).

282

The iron ball flies straight and true. When it hits the Snow Witch's globe, a bolt of white light shoots out from the globe towards you. *Test your Luck.* If you are Lucky, turn to **193**. If you are Unlucky, turn to **84**.

283

You breathe in deeply and walk stealthily behind the effigy towards the tunnel opposite (turn to **370**).

284

You only fall a few metres, landing on a grass-topped outcrop. You continue the arduous climb and it is not long before you reach the top of the mountain, which is covered by strange red vegetation. After the long climb, you sit down to rest and wait for the sunrise (turn to **217**).

285

The door opens into another tunnel which leads off into the distance. Stubb begins to complain about being tired and hungry, so you decide to sit down and rest. If you still have three portions of your Provisions, you eat one yourself and give one each to Redswift and Stubb. After resting for half an hour, you set off again and eventually the tunnel ends at a T-junction. If you wish to go left, turn to **298**. If you wish to go right, turn to **135**.

A huge, white-bearded man wearing white furs

286

The Barbarian's only interesting possessions are an engraved copper armband and a leather pouch containing three silver arrow heads. You take the arrow heads and look at the engraving on the armband. On it you can just read the words 'Strength is Power'. If you wish to wear the armband, turn to **293**. If you would rather place it in your pocket and continue walking up the gorge, turn to **319**.

287

If your *STAMINA* score is 10 or less, turn to **151**. If your *STAMINA* score exceeds 10, turn to **82**.

288

The tunnel soon leads into another cavern where you see a huge, white-bearded man wearing white furs, lifting a wooden chest on to a high shelf. He is a FROST GIANT. There is only one other exit out of his lair, via a tunnel in the opposite wall. If you wish to run through his lair into the tunnel opposite, turn to **243**. If you wish to attack him, turn to **112**.

289

Feeling tired after the strain of recent events, you sit down and rest. Stubb decides to go off to forage for food and Redswift begins to make a fire. You drift off into a deep sleep which your body welcomes. Add 2 *STAMINA* points. You are woken up an hour later by the ringing sound of clashing swords. You leap up and see Redswift engaged in combat with somebody wearing a hooded black cloak. When he turns, you realize he is a DARK ELF, the natural enemy of Redswift and his fellow wood elves. You run to help your friend but you are not needed. With a forward thrust of his sword, Redswift dispatches his adversary. 'Whose idea was it to wait for the boatman?' asks Redswift with a wry smile. Refusing to be baited, you suggest that you search through the belongings of the Dark Elf. A pouch on his belt contains a glass phial filled with a green liquid. Redswift takes out the stopper and sniffs it, but he does not recognize the smell. If you wish to drink the liquid, turn to **158**. If you would rather pour it on to the ground, turn to **173**.

290

You leave the cave and turn left, back into the tunnel, eating the cake as you go. It is stale and virtually tasteless, but gives you a little energy. Add 1 *STAMINA* point. Turn to **198**.

291

The Snow Witch stares at you again before making her choice. This time she calls out 'Star.' You smile and unfold your clenched fist, revealing the circular metal disc. You have outwitted her and she realizes the consequences. The globe starts to fill with white smoke and suddenly it shatters, the image of the Snow Witch disappears completely. Her shrill cry fills the cavern, but she is defeated. The three of you slap each other's hands in celebration. However, your joy is short-lived as you hear an ominous rumbling sound. The ground beneath your feet starts to tremble and huge cracks appear in the ice walls. The roof starts to cave in. Is this the chance to escape that the Snow Witch promised? *Test your Luck*. If you are Lucky, turn to **3**. If you are Unlucky, turn to **358**.

292

The Frost Giant turns to face you with the wooden chest raised above his head. He grunts with the effort and hurls the chest at you. *Test your Luck*. If you are Lucky, turn to **93**. If you are Unlucky, turn to **357**.

293

The armband is charmed with magical power. Add 1 *SKILL* point. You realize that you must hurry on up the gorge before the Death Spell runs its fatal course (turn to **319**).

294

The force of the Elemental picks you up and slams you against the wall, but luckily your backpack takes the brunt of the impact. Lose 2 *STAMINA* points. If you are still alive, turn to **372**.

295

None of the worshippers suspects that you are an intruder and you are able to walk through their temple without trouble, into the other tunnel (turn to **137**).

One of the Hill Trolls looks up and sees you walking by. He gives a cry of alarm and the three of them run out of the trees to attack. You have to fight two of them.

	SKILL	STAMINA
First HILL TROLL	8	9
Second HILL TROLL	9	9

Fight them both at the same time. During each Attack Round, they will both make a separate attack on you, but you must choose which one you will fight. Attack your chosen Hill Troll as in a normal battle. Against the other one you will throw for your Attack Strength in the normal way, but you will not wound it if your Attack Strength is greater; you must just count this as though you have defended yourself against its blow. Of course, if its Attack Strength is greater, it will wound you. If you defeat them both, turn to **164**.

When she smiles you see the tell-tale fangs

297

As you approach the sarcophagus, a woman's eerie laughter echoes round the chamber. A beautiful woman wearing white fur slowly rises out of the sarcophagus, and when she smiles you see the tell-tale fangs and realize with horror that the SNOW WITCH is a vampire! If you have some garlic, turn to **210**. If you do not have any garlic, turn to **60**.

298

The tunnel soon comes to a dead end. An ornate shield hangs from an iron nail on the end wall. If you wish to take the shield, turn to **183**. If you would rather turn round and walk down the tunnel past the last junction, turn to **135**.

299

The man nods his head and tells you to follow him. He walks towards the left-hand exit and points down the tunnel, telling you that the Snow Witch's chamber is at the end. If you wish to walk into the tunnel, turn to **214**. If you would rather draw your sword to attack him, turn to **156**.

300

You breathe in and stride confidently into the cavern, hoping not to attract attention. You walk behind the effigy towards the tunnel opposite. *Test your Luck.* If you are Lucky, turn to **295**. If you are Unlucky, turn to **370**.

301

You kneel down beside the water-hole and drink your fill of the cool water. However, the water-hole has been poisoned and you are soon gripping your stomach as the poison starts to take effect. Lose 4 *STAMINA* points. If you are still alive, turn to **96**.

302

Your head begins to spin and you get double vision. You stagger on, over the edge of the gorge, slipping and sliding on the loose stones. When your legs cannot support your weight any longer, you fall face down, and never get up. The Snow Witch's Death Spell has run its fatal course. Your adventure ends here.

303

The man you see before you is a MINSTREL. He is wearing a green and purple checked tunic over his hose and continues to play his lute despite your intrusion. Two large clay pots are the only other things in the cave. Will you:

Attack him with your sword?	Turn to **316**
Ask him about his music?	Turn to **80**
Nod politely and leave the cave to continue along the tunnel?	Turn to **111**

304

As you run past the globe, a bolt of white light shoots out from it, hitting you in the back. If your *STAMINA* total is 10 or less, turn to **44**. If it exceeds 10 in total, turn to **186**.

305

The wounded Mountain Elf calls out for mercy. If you wish to slay him, turn to **351**. If you wish to spare his life, turn to **204**.

306

You scramble out of the cave now that you know the Healer does not live there (turn to **355**).

307

The Illusionist laughs out loud – your sword merely cuts through one of his images and his dagger plunges into your shoulder. Lose 2 *STAMINA* points. Turn to **279**.

308

Fortunately it is not your sword-arm which is affected by frostbite, but nevertheless the blizzard has taken its toll. Lose 1 *SKILL* point and 3 *STAMINA* points. If you are still alive, turn to **174**.

309

As you withdraw your sword from the vile Brain Slayer you hear your two companions groaning as they slowly come round. They explain that the Brain Slayer drew them into the cavern and they were powerless to resist. You examine the chamber and see another door in the opposite wall. There are also two clay pots in a recess in the cavern wall, one red and one grey. Will you:

Open the door?	Turn to **176**
Look inside the red pot?	Turn to **101**
Look inside the grey pot?	Turn to **344**

310

As you walk along the edge of the crevasse, the wind starts to howl, blowing flurries of snow into your face. You put your head down and stride into the wind. A dark shape suddenly looms out of the curtain of snow – a huge hairy MAMMOTH stands before you, its long tusks curving out threateningly. Trumpeting loudly, it lumbers forward to attack.

MAMMOTH   *SKILL 10*   *STAMINA 11*

If you win, turn to **47**.

311

The tunnel ends at the edge of a pit, out of which a Dwarf is trying to climb, but he keeps on slipping back. The floor of the pit is covered with large ice boulders which have crashed down from a shaft above the pit. One lands on the Dwarf shoulders and you hear wild cheers from the top of the shaft as he tumbles on to the floor. The Dwarf sees you and shouts, 'Curse you, stranger, if you do not aid me. I see that you are not wearing a collar.' If you wish to help the Dwarf out of the pit, turn to **376**. If you would rather ignore his pleas and walk back to the junction, turn to **57**.

312

As you pull up the vine into the light, you see that it is crawling with revolting FLESH GRUBS, their blind heads writhing around in search of living flesh in which to burrow. You release the vine, but one of the Grubs crawls on to the back of your hand. Fortunately you manage to pull it off and stamp it underfoot. Add 1 *LUCK* point. You will not find the Healer in the tree stump so you decide to carry on walking up the river valley (turn to **119**).

313

As the White Dragon prepares to strike, you rub the copper ring vigorously. A warrior begins to take shape in front of you. Roll one die to see which warrior is summoned.

DIE ROLL	WARRIOR	SKILL	STAMINA
1	Knight	9	10
2	Barbarian	8	8
3	Dwarf	7	6
4	Elf	7	5
5	Ninja	6	6
6	Axeman	6	7

The summoned warrior will fight the White Dragon first.

WHITE DRAGON   *SKILL 12*   *STAMINA 14*

If the warrior wins the fight, he will disappear immediately (turn to **139**). If he loses, you must continue to fight yourself. If you win, turn to **139**.

314

You tug down hard on the rope, hoping that the Goblins are as stupid as they look. *Test your Luck.* If you are Lucky, turn to **188**. If you are Unlucky, turn to **86**.

315

The boatman jumps up and says, 'For 10 Gold Pieces, I'll ferry you all the way to Fang – jump aboard!' You pay the greedy boatman his money and he soon ferries you across the river. From the far bank you set off south across the Pagan Plain for Stonebridge, You have not been walking for long when you see dust rising in the distance. Redswift puts his ear to the ground and says, 'Horses or Centaurs, I can't tell which.' If you wish to wait and see who or what is approaching, turn to **180**. If you would rather lie down in the scrub to hide, turn to **58**.

316

As soon as you touch your sword, the Minstrel starts to play a strange high-pitched melody. You are immediately paralysed by the magic notes and can only watch helplessly as the Minstrel reaches into one of the pots to pull out a metal collar, an obedience collar, which he fits around your neck; now you will have to serve the Snow Witch for the rest of your life!

317

Despite being withered, the rose smells fresh and fragrant. As you inhale, you feel as though you are breathing new life into your lungs. Add 3 *STAMINA* points. If you have not done so already, you may:

Blow the flute	Turn to **74**
Read the runes on the stick	Turn to **345**
Read the book	Turn to **356**

If you do not wish to do any of the above, you may leave the cave and turn left into the tunnel (turn to **198**).

318

You hurl the orb as hard as you can down the tunnel. It shatters when it hits the ground, and there is a blinding flash of light followed by a ball of white heat which rushes up the tunnel. The heat is so intense that a scorching blast reaches you before you can move. Roll two dice and reduce your *STAMINA* by the total. If you are still alive, turn to **248**.

319

To your right you see a huge slab of rock; carved into it is the head of a fabulous bird surrounded by flames. Rough steps lead up the side of the rock slab to the mouth of a cave. If you wish to enter the cave, turn to **75**. If you would rather keep on walking up the gorge, turn to **161**.

320

The Wild Hill Man carried nothing of interest to you. However, the duck is ready to eat and you enjoy a delicious and nourishing feast. Add 4 *STAMINA* points. You may now either go back across the river over the rocks (turn to **364**); or follow a goat path up the side of the hill behind the clearing (turn to **231**).

321

You have only gone ten metres down the tunnel when the ice floor suddenly cracks and gives way under your weight. You fall down into an ice pit, a trap made by the Snow Witch's followers. Roll 1 die and deduct the number rolled from your *STAMINA* score. If you are still alive, turn to **254**.

322

Still suffering from the effects of the energy bolt, you have to decide quickly what to do next. Will you:

Use the sling again?	Turn to **216**
Try to smash the globe with your sword?	Turn to **244**
Try to *Escape*?	Turn to **262**

323

You soon arrive at an iron door which blocks your way forward. Beyond the iron door the tunnel turns to the right. If you possess a key, turn to **165**. If you do not possess a key, turn to **393**.

324

Although you get a headache, you are not injured by the fall. As you pick yourself up off the floor, you suddenly hear footsteps coming from the depths of the cave. In the distance you can see a swaying light and the vague outline of a hunched, sinewy figure who skulks slowly forward. If you wish to see who is coming towards you, turn to **37**. If you would rather run out of the cave, turn to **355**.

325

You notice that round its neck the Elf has a strange metal collar which glows in the semi-darkness of the tunnel. Suddenly it stops glowing and turns black. You wonder what is happening and decide to hurry on down the tunnel (turn to **241**).

326

You stumble to the right and accidentally step on one of the black footprints (turn to **87**).

327

You are now wearing an Amulet of Courage. Add 2 *SKILL* points. If you have not done so already, you may:

Blow the flute	Turn to **74**
Read the runes on the stick	Turn to **345**
Smell the rose	Turn to **317**

If you do not wish to do any of the above, you may leave the cave and turn left into the tunnel (turn to **198**).

A Pegasus will fly you anywhere for silver

328

You hand the Healer your silver object. He throws it through the crack and whistles loudly through his fingers. A few moments later you hear the noise of flapping wings outside and see the Healer smile briefly. Tie the silver to its mane and command it to take you to Firetop Mountain,' says the Healer. 'A Pegasus will fly you anywhere for silver. This is where we say goodbye. Good luck, I hope you make it.' You shake the Healer's hand, thanking him over and over again. Then, waving goodbye, you squeeze through the crack into the daylight. Before you stands a magnificent beast. It looks like a white stallion but it has wings. You tie the silver to its mane and climb on to its back. You shout your destination and suddenly you are flying through the air, clinging on to the neck of the mighty Pegasus. It is not long before you reach the mountain and land safely on the summit, which is covered in strange red vegetation. You jump down from the Pegasus and watch it fly off into the distance. You sit down to rest and wait for sunrise (turn to **217**).

329

Opening your backpack, you offer the Centaurs 10 Gold Pieces if they will take you to Stonebridge. Their leader's eyes light up at the sight of the gold and he realizes that you may be carrying lots more. Turn to **272**.

330

One of the daggers flies past your head, but the other sinks into your shoulder. Lose 2 *STAMINA* points. You stop briefly to pull the dagger out and throw it back at the Goblins before running painfully on (turn to **29**).

331

The Mountain Elf does not suspect that you are an intruder and you are able to walk casually past him (turn to **241**).

332

Redswift and Stubb pace around nervously, waiting for you to recover, and it is not long before their worst fears are realized. Three GOBLINS come running down the corridor, waving their swords and yelling for revenge. Despite the pain you are forced to join your friends in combat against one of the Goblins.

GOBLIN	*SKILL* 6	*STAMINA* 6

During this combat, reduce your *SKILL* by 3 points because of your injuries from the fireball. If you win, turn to **155**.

333

You instinctively clutch the hilt of your sword as the Healer's words of warning echo through your mind. Roll two dice and add 2 to the total. If the total is the same or less than your *SKILL* score, turn to **68**. If the total is greater than your *SKILL* score, turn to **185**.

334

The robed man tells you that he is a herbalist and has only just moved into the hut. You ask him guardedly if he has heard of a man called the Healer. He rubs his chin and shakes his head, saying, 'No, can't say that I have.' You decide to leave the herbalist, having already wasted too much of your limited time. Lose 1 *STAMINA* point. You walk back down the path and up the river valley (turn to **205**).

335

The bridge is quite narrow and very slippery. *Test your Luck*. If you are Lucky, turn to **41**. If you are Unlucky, turn to **389**.

336

You sit up and see that the Snow Witch's globe is cracked, but she appears to have come to no harm. She watches you carefully, ready for your next move (turn to **262**).

337

The snow is beginning to fall very heavily, swirling around in the strong wind. A blizzard is starting. If you wish to use your sword to dig a shelter in the snow, turn to **281**. If you would rather press on, turn to **229**.

338

You soon arrive at a crossroads in the tunnel. However, you have no time to examine the left and right branches, as a strange humanoid is advancing towards you from straight ahead (turn to **59**).

339

The tunnel runs straight on until it opens out into a

cavern. The walls are covered with ice and a large glass globe stands on an ice plinth in the centre. Suddenly an ORC runs into the cavern from the tunnel opposite and the globe immediately starts to radiate light. The outline of a face takes shape in the globe, one which you recognize – the Snow Witch! Her encased head starts to laugh and then you hear her speak. In a chilling voice she says, 'Although you killed me, you have not defeated me. My spirit can still defeat you. Watch carefully.' The Orc, who is standing by the globe, grips the metal collar round his neck and cries out, gasping for breath. His green face bulges as he desperately tries to stop the collar tightening. His efforts are futile and he soon falls silently to the floor. The Snow Witch's image sneers contemptuously and says, 'I have no use for servants any longer, and I know that two of you are still wearing my obedience collars. I will enjoy watching you die next, as a forerunner to the agony I have in store for your impudent warrior friend.' You refuse to watch Redswift and Stubb die helplessly, and you rack your brain to think of a way to overcome the spirit of the Snow Witch. Will you:

Try to smash the globe with your sword?	Turn to **244**
Fire an iron ball from your sling at the globe (if you have one)?	Turn to **216**
Try to run through the cavern into the opposite tunnel?	Turn to **304**

340

If the number you rolled was odd, the dart misses you but the whip curls itself around your left ankle, sending you crashing to the floor (turn to **108**). If the number you rolled was even, the whip misses you but the dart plunges into your arm. Lose 3 *STAMINA* points. If you are still able to run, turn to **177**.

341

When you open the door, one of the man's eyes flicks open. He seems, however, unconcerned at your intrusion and remains stretched out in his rocking-chair. If you wish to ask him if he is the Healer, turn to **71**. If you would rather just tell him you are lost, turn to **334**.

342

The only items you find that might be of use are a candle and a tinder-box. You take them and climb back down the ladder to continue walking east up the gorge (turn to **92**).

343

'Never mind,' says the Healer, 'you will just have to concentrate more. When you are ready, step across.' He tells you that the log is quite narrow and the pit is about 15 metres across. You take a deep breath and step on to the log and into the darkness. Roll two dice and add 2 to the total. If the total is the same or less than your *SKILL* score, turn to **91**. If the total is greater than your *SKILL* score, turn to **78**.

344

Lying at the bottom of the grey pot is an old parchment scroll with an unbroken wax seal. If you wish to break the seal and read the scroll, turn to **224**. If not, you may either look inside the red pot (turn to **101**), or leave the cavern by the door opposite (turn to **176**).

345

Your knowledge of runes is limited and you put the stick in your backpack, hoping to decipher it later. If you have not done so already, you may:

Blow the flute	Turn to **74**
Smell the rose	Turn to **317**
Read the book	Turn to **356**

If you do not wish to do any of the above, you may leave the cave and turn left into the tunnel (turn to **198**).

One of them suddenly lets out a shrill cry and swoops down to attack you

346

The herbalist was true to his word. The pills reduce the pain and you feel marginally better. Add 4 *STAMINA* points. Intent on finding the real Healer, you walk back down the path and up the river valley (turn to **205**).

347

You search through the clothing of the Goblins and find some salted fish, a candle and 2 Gold Pieces, which you decide to take, along with their daggers. The metal collars around their necks have stopped glowing, but you cannot remove them. After putting the Goblins' possessions in your backpack, you set off further down the tunnel (turn to **106**).

348

The flatness of the plain becomes monotonous and you forget to keep a constant lookout. The reflection of the sun on your armour has attracted a group of flying predators that you do not notice circling above you. They are green, with membranous wings, and they swoop down on their prey to kill them with their sharp claws. There are four of these BIRD-MEN above you and one of them suddenly lets out a shrill cry and swoops down to attack you. *Test your Luck.* If you are Lucky, turn to **256**. If you are Unlucky, turn to **369**.

349

You fall a couple of metres only before landing on an icy ledge protruding from the side of the crevasse. You are lucky to escape with only a twisted ankle. Lose 1 *STAMINA* point. Using your sword, you cut hand- and toe-holds into the side of the crevasse and haul yourself up. Plodding your way through the thick snow, you continue your quest (turn to **212**).

350

The Rattlesnake bites the leg of your boot and empties its poison harmlessly on to the hardened leather. With one swipe of your sword, you cut off its head and continue your trek up the gorge (turn to **252**).

351

Continue your sword fight to the bitter end.

MOUNTAIN ELF   *SKILL 6*   *STAMINA 2*

If you win, turn to **325**.

352

The iron ball flies through the air but whistles past the Frost Giant's head. You have no time to reload and must rely on your sword-arm again (turn to **292**).

353

Redswift draws the short straw and reaches for the handle. Just as he is about to touch it he draws his hand away, his elfin intuition telling him that there is a trap. He inspects the casket more closely and finds a hidden catch underneath the handle. He presses it with his finger and the lid clicks open. Inside the casket is a pair of grey skin boots. 'Boots of the elder elves,' he says with glee, 'what treasure – nobody knows how to make these any more. No matter what surface you are walking on, no one will hear you, if you are wearing these boots. Let us draw lots again to decide who shall wear them.' If you roll a 1 or 2, turn to **203**. If you roll a 3 or 4, turn to **265**. If you roll a 5 or 6, turn to **379**.

354

Inside the backpack you find a pair of old leather sandals, a stuffed rat and a mouldy loaf. If you wish to eat the loaf, turn to **247**. If you would prefer to leave the cave immediately through the tunnel opposite, turn to **221**.

355

Half-running, half-sliding, you land back on the floor of the gorge. However, you are getting weaker by the minute. Lose 1 *STAMINA* point. Walking uphill, you follow the gorge east (turn to **377**).

356

Flicking up the clasp which keeps the book shut, a tiny hidden needle grazes your finger. There is poison on its tip to trap unwary thieves. Lose 4 *STAMINA* points. If you are still alive, you may open the book (turn to **97**) or, if you have not done so already, you may:

Blow the flute	Turn to **74**
Read the runes on the stick	Turn to **345**
Smell the rose	Turn to **317**

If you do not wish to do any of the above, you may leave the cave and turn left into the tunnel (turn to **198**).

357

You react slowly to the improvised missile and the full force of the flying chest hits you in the stomach. You are winded and stagger back against the wall. Lose 2 *STAMINA* points. The Frost Giant lumbers towards you intent on finishing you off.

MOUNTAIN ELF   *SKILL* 10   *STAMINA* 10

During each round of combat you must reduce your Attack Strength by 2 because you are winded. You may Escape after two Attack Rounds by running out of his lair into the next tunnel (turn to **338**). If you win, turn to **45**.

358

A massive lump of ice crashes down on top of you. Lose 4 *STAMINA* points. If you are still alive, turn to **90**.

359

The Healer takes the egg from you and breaks off the top of the shell. He takes some powder out of a pendant hanging round his neck, and pours it into the egg. After stirring it with a stick, he hands it to you, telling you to drink it. You swallow the raw egg concoction, trusting the Healer's knowledge. He then tells you to walk ahead of him (turn to **154**).

360

Once again the current drags you under the surface of the water. This time the weight of the gold in your backpack keeps you under, because you are too weak to swim. Your adventure ends here.

361

Lose 1 *LUCK* point. Turn to **127**.

362

The horned helmet fits you perfectly and it is a fine addition to your armour. Add 1 *SKILL* point. Red-swift takes the Centaur's spear, before the three of you set off for Stonebridge (turn to **278**).

363

You make your way slowly up the mountain until you reach a rock face that is too steep to climb. You walk round the side until you see a massive wall of ice which completely blocks a gully between two peaks of the mountain – the glacier. Your heart leaps as you catch sight of the piece of fur left hanging on the wall of ice by the trapper. Although you cannot see the entrance, you walk straight ahead. You shut your eyes as you think you are about to walk into the wall of ice, but you walk straight through the illusion and find yourself inside a long tunnel carved into the ice. You walk down it and soon arrive at a T-junction. If you wish to turn left, turn to **395**. If you wish to turn right, turn to **215**.

364

You manage to hop over the rocks without falling into the river. However, the Death Spell continues to take its toll. Lose 1 *STAMINA* point. You turn right and walk up the river valley (turn to **115**).

They are trapped by the hypnotic powers of the Brain Slayer

365

The tunnel ends at a door which swings open before you even touch it. You look into a cavern and are surprised to see Redswift and Stubb kneeling in submission to a horrible robed creature with an octopus-like head. Two of its tentacles are wrapped around your friends' heads and they are trapped by the hypnotic powers of the BRAIN SLAYER. If you are wearing an Amulet of Courage, turn to **189**. If you are not wearing this item, turn to **126**.

366

You search through the clothing of the Goblins and find some salted fish, a candle and 2 Gold Pieces which you decide to keep. Both Goblins are wearing metal collars round their necks which you cannot remove. Taking the dagger, from the Goblin you slew, you cut hand- and toe-holds into the side of the pit and haul yourself up. Picking up your sword, you decide which way to head, wondering if there are any more traps further down the tunnel. If you wish to continue down it, turn to **88**. If you would rather walk back to where the tunnel forked and turn left along the other branch, turn to **29**.

367

You try to stand up, but your legs feel as stiff and heavy as iron. You look at Redswift; he also tries to stand up, alas without success. As you begin to lose consciousness, you realize that the Snow Witch has had her revenge. Your adventure ends here.

368

The tunnel ends at a wooden door which is locked. You press your ear to it and hear the sound of feet slowly shuffling across the floor. If you wish to knock on the door, turn to **83**. If you would rather return to the junction and head straight on, turn to **150**.

369

You are slow in drawing your sword and the BIRD-MAN is able to rip you with its claws. Lose 2 *STAMINA* points. You watch as it climbs into the sky but you are now ready to meet it as it dives down again to attack.

BIRD-MAN   *SKILL* 12   *STAMINA* 8

If you win, turn to **18**.

370

You are almost at the entrance to the tunnel when the worshippers stop their chanting. They stand up and one of them calls out to you asking why you did not stop to sing the praises of The Frozen One. If you have a magic flute, you can tell them that you have been ordered to go and play it for the Snow Witch (turn to **31**). Otherwise you may either fight them (turn to **143**), or try to run for the tunnel (turn to **33**).

371

Before you can reach the safety of the outcrop, the avalanche descends upon you, sweeping you down the mountain. *Test your Luck*. If you are Lucky, turn to **257**. If you are Unlucky, turn to **64**.

372

The Elemental disappears as quickly as it appeared, and all is calm again. Although quite badly injured, Redswift and Stubb are still alive. Despite his pain, Stubb manages to make a sarcastic remark about your rash desire to touch everything in sight. Ignoring his jibe, you sling the shield on to your arm (add 1 *SKILL* point) and walk together back down the tunnel and past the last junction (turn to **135**).

373

You place an iron ball in the sling and twirl it around your head before releasing it at the Frost Giant. Roll two dice. If the number of the total is the same or less than your *SKILL* score, turn to **12**. If the total is higher than your *SKILL* score, turn to **352**.

374

Barbarians are used to people creeping up on them, and the noise of your boots on the stony ground wakes him up. Barbarians also fight first and ask questions later. He jumps up and grabs his battleaxe to attack you.

BARBARIAN   *SKILL* 9   *STAMINA* 8

If you win, turn to **286**.

375

You curse as the iron ball misses its target. Lose 1 *LUCK* point. A bolt of white light shoots out from the globe, hitting you in the chest. If your *STAMINA* total is 10 or less, turn to **44**. If it exceeds 10 in total, turn to **122**.

376

You lie down and lean over the edge of the pit, and tell the Dwarf to grab your arm. Much to the annoyance of the spectators above, the Dwarf escapes from the pit. You run together back to the junction where the Dwarf turns right. You tell the Dwarf that you intend to carry straight on to find the Snow Witch, as turning right will lead you back to the hall of worship. The Dwarf tells you that he must escape quickly and return to his village now that he is free. He thanks you for helping him and hands you a leather bag, then runs off; but before he disappears, he turns and shouts, 'Beware the White Rat.' You open the leather bag and find a sling and three iron balls. You pack them away and set off along the tunnel (turn to **125**).

377

You get very tired walking up the gorge and do not pay attention to where you are treading. You accidentally step on a RATTLESNAKE, which strikes at you with its deadly fangs. *Test your Luck*. If you are Lucky, turn to **350**. If you are Unlucky, turn to **167**.

378

You draw your sword and lunge at the huge white beast.

YETI   *SKILL* 11   *STAMINA* 12

If you win, turn to **67**.

379

You draw the short straw and cheer at your good fortune. Add 1 *LUCK* point. You kick off your old boots and put on the magical elfin boots. Striding off down the corridor without making the slightest sound, you cheerfully lead the way, and your jealous-looking companions follow (turn to **20**).

380

The Snow Witch is strong and she manages to snatch the stick from your hand and throw it on to the floor. Her gaze intensifies and your mind comes completely under her control. You loosen your collar and bare your neck in readiness for her to drink your blood. You will be her servant forever in the world of the undead.

381

The weight of the gold in your backpack keeps dragging you underwater. If you wish to take off your backpack, turn to **42**. If you would rather keep it on and struggle to breathe, turn to **287**.

382

As you draw your sword, the MOUNTAIN ELF, with a shrill battle-cry, pulls back his cloak and grips his sword.

MOUNTAIN ELF   *SKILL 6*   *STAMINA 6*

If you win, turn to **208**.

383

By the time all three of you have run through the acid shower, you are very demoralized. Lose 1 *LUCK* point. Nevertheless, you press on resolutely (turn to **339**).

384

You pull down the hood of your cloak as far as possible and walk towards the tunnel exit on your right. *Test your Luck.* If you are Lucky, turn to **295**. If you are Unlucky, turn to **370**.

385

You feel yourself growing weaker by the minute. Lose 1 *STAMINA* point. Ahead you see a gorge running east between two hills and you decide that you may as well walk up it, in the hope of finding the Healer. Half-way up the left-hand side of the gorge you see the entrance to a cave. If you wish to climb up to the cave, turn to **170**. If you would rather keep walking up the gorge, turn to **377**.

386

You are unable to move out of the path of the dagger quickly enough and it cuts a deep gash in your side. Lose 2 *STAMINA* points. You have no time to recover as the Goblin raises his arm to strike you again. You must fight him with your bare hands.

GOBLIN   *SKILL* 5   *STAMINA* 5

During each Attack Round you must reduce your Attack Strength by 3 as you are without your sword. If you win, turn to **43**.

387

The cold is almost unbearable. Your hands and feet are numb and you wonder if you will be able to grip your sword should danger arise. By the time the blizzard finally dies down, you realize that you should have taken shelter; one of your hands has become frostbitten. *Test your Luck*. If you are Lucky, turn to **308**. If you are Unlucky, turn to **225**.

388

As you walk along, the Elf introduces himself. 'My name is Redswift, and he is known as Stubb,' he says, pointing to the smiling Dwarf. 'We met here as slaves in the service of the vile Snow Witch. We both now hope to return to our villages. I live in the Moonstone Hills and Stubb comes from Stonebridge. If we manage to escape from these infernal caverns, you are more than welcome to come and stay with us. Stonebridge is on the way to my village in the hills. It's also a long way off.' Just as Redswift is about to continue, you notice something strange about the floor and tell them to look down. There are two pairs of parallel footsteps running down the tunnel for approximately 20 metres. One pair is painted white and the other is painted black. You wonder why they are there, but cannot come up with an answer. Will you:

Walk on the white footprints?	Turn to **11**
Walk on the black footprints?	Turn to **87**
Walk between the footprints?	Turn to **220**

389

You are almost over the bridge when you suddenly slip and fall over the edge. *Test your Luck*. If you are Lucky, turn to **349**. If you are Unlucky, turn to **197**.

390

You draw your sword and advance towards the old man, asking him why he is so eager to acquire blood-money. You pin him against the wall holding the point of your sword under his chin and ask him to explain why a so-called philanthropic Healer requires 50 Gold Pieces for saving a life. The old man starts to tremble and says, 'All right, I'm sorry, I'm not the Healer. I am only a simple herbalist, down on my luck. I figured that soon you wouldn't be needing your gold anyhow, so you wouldn't mind me having some of it. I realize that it was a foolish thing to do. Listen, you can have some of my own pills that stop my aches and pains. They might help. No charge of course.' With your sword tip still pinning him up against the wall, he reaches into his robes and pulls out a small bottle. He opens it and hands you three green pills. You grab the pills and leave the hut, telling the old man that he is lucky to be alive. Outside, you have to decide what to do. If you wish to swallow the pills, turn to **346**. If you would rather walk back down the path and up the river valley, turn to **205**.

391

If you have frostbite in your sword-arm, turn to **195**. If not, turn to **249**.

392

The Snow Witch stares at you for a long time before calling out 'Circle.' Terror spreads across your face as you unfold your fist, revealing the star-shaped metal disc. The Snow Witch laughs and another energy bolt shoots out from her globe. It slams into your chest, killing you instantly. Your adventure is over.

393

You are trapped inside the mountain tunnels. You know that it will not be long before the Snow Witch's guards discover you and condemn you to a life of slavery. You have failed in your mission.

394

As you climb down inside the dark depths of the hollow tree, you suddenly feel cold, clammy, maggot-like larvae slithering up the vine. They are as big as your finger and they crawl on to your body and bare arms, but you cannot brush them off for fear of falling. In the dark, you don't see their blind heads writhing about, but you feel the pain when one burrows its hook-like teeth into your arm. You are covered with FLESH GRUBS. In blind panic, you try to haul yourself up the vine, the effect of the Death Spell making it a terrible effort. If your *STAMINA* is 6 or less, turn to **191**. If your *STAMINA* is greater than 6, turn to **222**.

395

The tunnel bends round to the right. As you turn the corner you almost bump into a tall pale-skinned humanoid coming the other way. He is wearing a white cloak with a hood pulled over his head. He is a MOUNTAIN ELF, one of the Snow Witch's followers. Will you:

Nod your head at him and walk by nonchalantly?	Turn to **89**
Tell him you have come to join the Snow Witch's followers?	Turn to **274**
Attack him with your sword?	Turn to **17**

396

The writing fades away before you have time to read it. Lose 1 *LUCK* point. If you have not done so already, you may either look inside the red pot (turn to **101**) or leave the cavern by the door opposite (turn to **176**).

⚀ ⚂

You draw your sword as it reaches for its axe

397

The Elf sees you draw your sword and advance towards him. He calmly strings his bow and fires an arrow at you with deadly accuracy. Redswift's brother is an expert bowman: his arrow kills you instantly when it pierces your heart.

398

As you climb the rope-ladder, you hear the noise of shuffling feet on the platform above you. You climb through a hole in the platform, but you are not greeted by the Healer – you have intruded into the hideaway of a vicious MAN-ORC. You draw your sword as it reaches for its axe.

MAN-ORC **SKILL 8** **STAMINA 6**

If you win, turn to **342**.

399

Stubb wakes you in the middle of the night after completing the second watch. The rest of the night passes peacefully and in the morning you are able to continue your journey to Stonebridge (turn to **13**).

400

It is the beginning of a beautiful day. A day which is probably going to be the most enjoyable of your life. The spirit of the evil Snow Witch has been destroyed and you are cured of her terrible curse. As you climb down the mountain, you think about the kind; unselfish Healer, and of your friends Redswift and Stubb. You are suddenly eager to meet the jolly old Dwarf again and set off towards Stonebridge as fast as you can, hoping that he will have returned from Darkwood Forest. You have earned yourself a welcome rest, although whether or not you will get it is another story...

HOW TO FIGHT
THE CREATURES OF
THE ICEFINGER MOUNTAINS

Before embarking on your adventure, you must first determine your own strengths and weaknesses. You have in your possession a sword and a backpack containing provisions (food and drink) for the trip. You have been preparing for your quest by training yourself in swordplay and exercising vigorously to build up your stamina.

To see how effective your preparations have been, you must use the dice to determine your initial *SKILL* and *STAMINA* scores. On pages 212-213 there is an *Adventure Sheet* which you may use to record the details of an adventure. On it you will find boxes for recording your *SKILL* and *STAMINA* scores.

You are advised to either record your scores on the *Adventure Sheet* in pencil, or make photocopies of the page to use in future adventures.

SKILL, STAMINA AND LUCK

- Roll one die. Add 6 to this number and enter this total in the *SKILL* box on the *Adventure Sheet*.
- Roll both dice. Add 12 to the number rolled and enter this total in the *STAMINA* box.
- There is also a *LUCK* box. Roll one die, add 6 to this number and enter this total in the *LUCK* box.

For reasons that will be explained below, *SKILL*, *STAMINA* and *LUCK* scores change constantly during an adventure. You must keep an accurate record of these scores and for this reason you are advised either to write small in the boxes or to keep an eraser handy. But never rub out your *Initial* scores., Although you may be awarded additional *SKILL*, *STAMINA* and *LUCK* points, these totals may never exceed your *Initial* scores except on very rare occasions, when you will be instructed on a particular page.

Your *SKILL* score reflects your swordsmanship and general fighting expertise; the higher the better. Your *STAMINA* score reflects your general constitution, your will to survive, your determination and overall fitness; the higher your *STAMINA* score, the longer you will be able to survive. Your *LUCK* score indicates how naturally lucky a person you are. *LUCK* – and magic – are facts of life in the fantasy kingdom you are about to explore.

BATTLES

You will often come across pages in the book which instruct you to fight a creature of some sort. An option to flee may be given, but if not – or if you choose to attack the creature anyway – you must resolve the battle as described below.

First record the creature's *SKILL* and *STAMINA* scores in the first vacant Monster Encounter Box on your *Adventure Sheet*. The scores for each creature

The sequence of combat is then:

1. Roll both dice once for the creature. Add its *SKILL* score. This total is the creature's Attack Strength.
2. Roll both dice once for yourself. Add the number rolled to your current *SKILL* score. This total is your Attack Strength.
3. If your Attack Strength is higher than that of the creature, you have wounded it. Proceed to step 4. If the creature's Attack Strength is higher than yours, it has wounded you. Proceed to step 5 both Attack Strength if totals are the same, you have avoided each other's blows – start the next Attack Round from step 1 above.
4. You have wounded the creature, so subtract 2 points from its *STAMINA* score. You may use your *LUCK* here to do additional damage (see next page).

5. The creature has wounded you, so subtract 2 points from your own *STAMINA* score. Again you may use LUCK at this stage (see next page).

6. Make the appropriate adjustments to either the creature's or your own *STAMINA* scores (and your *LUCK* score if you used *LUCK* – see next page).

7. Begin the next Attack Round by returning to your current *SKILL* score and repeating steps 1-6. This sequence continues until the *STAMINA* score of either you or the creature you are fighting has been reduced to zero (death).

ESCAPING

On some pages you may be given the option of running away from a battle should things be going badly for you. However, if you do run away, the creature automatically gets in one wound on you (subtract 2 *STAMINA* points) as you flee. Such is the price of cowardice. Note that you may use *LUCK* on this wound in the normal way (see below). You may only *Escape* if that option is specifically given to you on the page.

FIGHTING MORE THAN ONE CREATURE

If you come across more than one creature in a particular encounter, the instructions on that page will tell you how to handle the battle. Sometimes you will treat them as a single monster; sometimes you will fight each one in turn.

LUCK

At various times during your adventure, either in battles or when you come across situations in which you could either be lucky or unlucky (details of these are given on the pages themselves), you may call on your *LUCK* to make the outcome more favourable. But beware! Using *LUCK* is a risky business, and if you are unlucky, the results could be disastrous.

The procedure for using your *LUCK* is as follows: roll two dice. If the number rolled is equal to or less than your current *LUCK* score, you have been lucky and the result will go in your favour. If the number rolled is higher than your current *LUCK* score, you have been unlucky and you will be penalized.

This procedure is known as *Testing your Luck*. Each time you *Test your Luck*, you must subtract one point from your current *LUCK* score. Thus you will soon realize that the more you rely on your *LUCK*, the more risky this will become.

Using Luck in Battles

On certain pages of the book you will be told to *Test your Luck* and will be told the consequences of your being lucky or unlucky. However, in battles, you always have the option of using your *LUCK* either to inflict a more serious wound on a creature you have just wounded, or to minimize the effects of a wound, the creature has just inflicted on you.

If you have just wounded the creature, you may *Test your Luck* as described above. If you are Lucky, you have inflicted a severe wound and may subtract an extra 2 points from the creature's *STAMINA* score. However, if you are Unlucky, the wound was a mere graze and you must restore 1 point to the creature's *STAMINA* (i.e. instead of scoring the normal 2 points of damage, you have now scored only 1.

If the creature has just wounded you, you may *Test your Luck* to try to minimize the wound. If you are Lucky, you have managed to avoid the full damage of the blow. Restore 1 point of *STAMINA* (i.e. instead of doing 2 points of damage it has done only 1). If you are Unlucky, you have taken a more serious blow. Subtract 1 extra *STAMINA* point.

Remember that you must subtract 1 point from your *LUCK* score every time you *Test your Luck*.

RESTORING SKILL, STAMINA AND LUCK

Skill

Your *SKILL* score will not change much during your adventure. Occasionally, a page may give instructions to increase or decrease your *SKILL* score. A Magic Weapon may increase your *SKILL*, but remember that only one weapon can be used at a time! You cannot claim 2 *SKILL* bonuses for carrying two Magic Swords. Your *SKILL* score can never exceed its *Initial* value. Drinking the Potion of *SKILL* (see later) will restore your *SKILL* to its *Initial* level at any time.

Stamina and Provisions

Your *STAMINA* score will change a lot during your adventure as you fight monsters and undertake arduous tasks. As you near your goal, your *STAMINA* level may be dangerously low and battles may be particularly risky, so be careful!

Your backpack contains enough Provisions for ten meals. You may rest and eat at any time except when engaged in a Battle. Eating a meal restores 4 *STAMINA* points. When you eat a meal, add 4 points to your *STAMINA* score and deduct 1 point from your Provisions. A separate Provisions

Remaining box is provided on the *Adventure Sheet* for recording details of Provisions. Remember that you have a long way to go, so use your Provisions wisely!

Remember also that your *STAMINA* score may never exceed its *Initial* value. Drinking the Potion of Strength (see later) will restore your *STAMINA* to its *Initial* level at any time.

Luck

Additions to your *LUCK* score are awarded through the adventure when you have been particularly lucky. Details are given on the pages of this book. Remember that, as with *SKILL* and *STAMINA*, your *LUCK* score may never exceed its *Initial* value. Drinking the Potion of Fortune (see later) will restore your *LUCK* to its *Initial* level at any time, and increase your *Initial LUCK* by 1 point.

EQUIPMENT AND POTIONS

You will start your adventure with a bare minimum of equipment, but you may find or buy other items during your travels. You are armed with a sword and are dressed in leather armour. You have a backpack to hold you Provisions and any treasures you may come across.

In addition, you may take one bottle of a magic potion which will aid you on your quest. You .may choose to take a bottle of any of the following:

A Potion of *SKILL* – restores *SKILL* points

A Potion of Strength – restores *STAMINA* points

A Potion of Fortune – restores *LUCK* points and adds 1 to *Initial LUCK*

These potions may be taken at any time during your adventure (except when engaged in a Battle). Taking a measure of potion will restore *SKILL*, *STAMINA* or *LUCK* scores to their *Initial* level (and the Potion of Fortune will add 1 point to your *Initial LUCK* score before *LUCK* is restored).

Each bottle of potion contains enough for *one* measure, i.e. the characteristic may be restored once during an adventure. Make a note on your *Adventure Sheet* when you have used up a potion.

Remember also that you may only choose *one* of the three potions to take on your trip, so choose wisely!

HINTS ON PLAY

Your journey will be perilous and you are likely to fail on your first attempt. Make notes and draw a map as you explore – this map will be invaluable in future adventures and enable you to progress rapidly through to unexplored sections.

Not all areas contain treasure; many merely contain traps and creatures which you will no doubt fall foul of. You may make wrong turnings during your quest and while you may indeed progress through to your ultimate destination, it is by no means certain that you will find what you are searching for.

It will be realized that entries make no sense if read in numerical order. It is essential that you read only the entries you are instructed to read. Reading other entries will only cause confusion and may lessen the excitement during play.

The one true way involves a minimum of risk and any player, no matter how weak on initial dice rolls, should be able to get through fairly easily.

May the luck of the gods go with you on the adventure ahead!

ADVENTURE SHEET

SKILL	STAMINA	LUCK

BACKPACK ITEMS:

GOLD:

JEWELS:

POTIONS:

PROVISIONS:

ENEMY ENCOUNTER SHEET

SKILL ☐ STAMINA ☐	SKILL ☐ STAMINA ☐	SKILL ☐ STAMINA ☐	SKILL ☐ STAMINA ☐
SKILL ☐ STAMINA ☐	SKILL ☐ STAMINA ☐	SKILL ☐ STAMINA ☐	SKILL ☐ STAMINA ☐
SKILL ☐ STAMINA ☐	SKILL ☐ STAMINA ☐	SKILL ☐ STAMINA ☐	SKILL ☐ STAMINA ☐
SKILL ☐ STAMINA ☐	SKILL ☐ STAMINA ☐	SKILL ☐ STAMINA ☐	SKILL ☐ STAMINA ☐
SKILL ☐ STAMINA ☐	SKILL ☐ STAMINA ☐	SKILL ☐ STAMINA ☐	SKILL ☐ STAMINA ☐
SKILL ☐ STAMINA ☐	SKILL ☐ STAMINA ☐	SKILL ☐ STAMINA ☐	SKILL ☐ STAMINA ☐

ADVENTUIRE SHEET

| SKILL | | STAMINA | | LUCK | |

BACKPACK ITEMS:

GOLD:

JEWELS:

POTIONS:

PROVISIONS:

ENEMY ENCOUNTER SHEET

SKILL ☐ STAMINA ☐	SKILL ☐ STAMINA ☐	SKILL ☐ STAMINA ☐	SKILL ☐ STAMINA ☐
SKILL ☐ STAMINA ☐	SKILL ☐ STAMINA ☐	SKILL ☐ STAMINA ☐	SKILL ☐ STAMINA ☐
SKILL ☐ STAMINA ☐	SKILL ☐ STAMINA ☐	SKILL ☐ STAMINA ☐	SKILL ☐ STAMINA ☐
SKILL ☐ STAMINA ☐	SKILL ☐ STAMINA ☐	SKILL ☐ STAMINA ☐	SKILL ☐ STAMINA ☐
SKILL ☐ STAMINA ☐	SKILL ☐ STAMINA ☐	SKILL ☐ STAMINA ☐	SKILL ☐ STAMINA ☐
SKILL ☐ STAMINA ☐	SKILL ☐ STAMINA ☐	SKILL ☐ STAMINA ☐	SKILL ☐ STAMINA ☐

ADVENTURE SHEET

SKILL	STAMINA	LUCK

BACKPACK ITEMS:

GOLD:

JEWELS:

POTIONS:

PROVISIONS:

ENEMY ENCOUNTER SHEET

SKILL ☐ STAMINA ☐	SKILL ☐ STAMINA ☐	SKILL ☐ STAMINA ☐	SKILL ☐ STAMINA ☐
SKILL ☐ STAMINA ☐	SKILL ☐ STAMINA ☐	SKILL ☐ STAMINA ☐	SKILL ☐ STAMINA ☐
SKILL ☐ STAMINA ☐	SKILL ☐ STAMINA ☐	SKILL ☐ STAMINA ☐	SKILL ☐ STAMINA ☐
SKILL ☐ STAMINA ☐	SKILL ☐ STAMINA ☐	SKILL ☐ STAMINA ☐	SKILL ☐ STAMINA ☐
SKILL ☐ STAMINA ☐	SKILL ☐ STAMINA ☐	SKILL ☐ STAMINA ☐	SKILL ☐ STAMINA ☐
SKILL ☐ STAMINA ☐	SKILL ☐ STAMINA ☐	SKILL ☐ STAMINA ☐	SKILL ☐ STAMINA ☐

YOU ARE THE HERO

FIGHTING FANTASY

DEATHTRAP DUNGEON

IAN LIVINGSTONE

Devised by the devilish mind of Baron Sukumvit, the
labyrinth of Fang plays host to the Trial of Champions
– a challenge that no adventurer every survived. You'll
have to pit your wits against some fiendish foes if you
have any hope of seeing daylight again...

YOU ARE THE HERO

FIGHTING FANTASY

THE

FOREST

OF

DOOM

IAN LIVINGSTONE

A war is raging and your help is needed to vanquish
the evil trolls. To save the dwarfs, you must find the
grand wizard Yaztromo and track down the pieces of a
legendary war hammer lost in the depths of Darkwood
Forest, where gruesome monsters lurk...

YOU ARE THE HERO

CREATURE
OF
HAVOC

STEVE
JACKSON

You must stop the march to power of the evil
necromancer Zharradan Marr. You'll need to fight your
way on board flying ship the Galleykeep if you have any
hope of defeating his brand of black magic...

YOU ARE THE HERO

FIGHTING FANTASY

ISLAND OF THE LIZARD KING

IAN LIVINGSTONE

The village of Oyster Bay has been overpowered by
Lizard Men and its people forced into back-breaking
toil in the gold mines of Fire Island. You must set
sail to free them – but first you'll need to defeat the
Lizard King himself and he has only one, top-secret
weakness...

YOU ARE THE HERO

ASSASSINS
— OF —
ALLANSIA

IAN
LIVINGSTONE

After accepting a challenge to survive on Snake Island,
a nightmare unfolds when a bounty is placed on your
head. Beware the ruthless assassins hell bent on
hunting you down – but who are they? Where are they?
Trust no-one...

YOU ARE · THE HERO

FIGHTING FANTASY

COLLECT THEM ALL, BRAVE ADVENTURER!